A STORM OF FIRE AND ICE

HAVEN ACADEMY: BOOK 3

ARIEL RENNER

CONTENTS

AUTHOR'S NOTE

While this book can be read as a standalone novel, it contains spoilers for the following books:

- *Fated to the Fire Enemy (Athenaeum Academy: Book 1)*

- *Forbidden Ice Prince (Haven Academy: Book 1)*

- *Taken by the Storm Prince (Haven Academy: Book 2)*

I recommend you read them first to experience the story as intended. They are available on Amazon and at: **arielrenner.com/books**

Enjoy!

Ariel Renner

PROLOGUE
HELENA

I rubbed my hands together vigorously, desperately trying to generate the slightest bit of heat. The entire fucking castle was made of ice. Yes, it's called the Ice Kingdom for a reason, but seriously?! I didn't even know such things existed outside of Disney movies.

Cupping my hands together, I blew an orange ribbon of flame into my palms, bringing some miniscule source of warmth to my frozen bones. As I glanced out the window, endless snowdrifts blanketed the landscape of this unfamiliar place. All I wanted was to see green grass again.

Things would be greener—warmer—if we'd gone to the Earth Kingdom for winter break.

I shook the thought away and reminded myself why I was really there. Because Fannar needed me.

He perched awkwardly on his bed, his face rigid and expressionless as he stared into nothingness. His elbows rested firmly on his knees with his fingers interlocked at the front of his face. His left foot tapped restlessly against the smooth floor. Tiny snowflakes hovered around him in the air, attempting to cocoon him in an icy aura.

Maybe *he* was the one freezing the room? As if it needed to be any colder!

"Fannar. Babe!" I pleaded with him. "We don't need more ice, please!"

Fannar's arctic blue eyes blinked up at me, like I'd disturbed his thoughts. "Sorry, Helena," he murmured. He stretched his back a little and huffed out a sigh.

The duvet on his bed crunched underneath me as I sat beside him, frosty from his powers spreading out around him.

"Still worried about your sister?" I asked.

Fannar nodded. His familiar icy expression revealed nothing, but I'd learned to read the tiny hint of emotion that his eyes betrayed.

"Every day that we're sitting around here, Gwyneira is trapped in the Storm Castle. Gods know what that monster is doing to her, Helena." He clenched his fists, and more ice collected on them. "We don't know if she's okay, if she's alive. Even Mother and Father don't know anything."

"How is it that they've seriously not checked on her once?" I snapped.

He shook his head. “Gwyneira is nothing more than a tool to them. Always has been.” He paused and smiled humorlessly at me. “My parents would treat you the same way if they weren’t so damn scared of you.”

“That’s me. Scary Fire Enchanted from the Unenchanted Realm.” I grinned and shrugged, but Fannar hung his head again. I placed my hand on his. “Well, then, it’s up to us to save her.”

Fannar paused, contemplating my words. “It could start a war.”

“So what?” I scoffed. “You’re the future king of the Ice Kingdom. You have every right to rescue your sister if the prince is being cruel to her.”

As the words left my mouth, I knew I had him. Fannar was always so soft-hearted when it came to Gwyneira. He looked at me with pleading eyes, silently asking me for permission to rescue his sister.

“What’s the plan?” I smirked, knowing that I had won this battle. “I’m sure you’ve already thought about it.”

Fannar’s eyes lit up. “She has to be inside the Storm Castle. We can sneak in and look for her. Gwyneira doesn’t have powers, or if she does now, she won’t know how to use them. She’s completely defenseless, so if we escape with her without anyone noticing, that would be best.”

"If we're caught, the Storm Prince won't let her go without a fight." I slammed my fist down onto the palm of my other hand with a loud smack.

"Then we'll deal with him. We're two of the most powerful students at the academy. That has to count for something, right?"

I nodded, eying him cautiously. "But, by 'deal with him', you mean . . . ?"

Fannar's eyes and tone darkened. "If he resists, I'll kill him."

CHAPTER ONE
GWYNEIRA

I know it's here somewhere.

A cool night breeze played with my long white hair as I stood at the edge of the terrace adjoining the royal chambers that Brontes and I shared, peering at the night sky through a large telescope. My heart fluttered with anticipation as I adjusted the lens, focusing on the dazzling diamond-studded canvas above me.

And there it was—the constellation Luminaria. It glimmered against the indigo sky, its celestial light a guiding beacon in the dark. I traced the pattern of stars with my gaze, each point of light a distant world teeming with possibility and wonder.

"Are you almost ready for bed, snowflake?" Brontes asked as he walked onto the terrace.

"Brontes, I found it!" I exclaimed, looking up from the telescope. "I found Luminaria!"

Warm light spilled out from the open doorway to our chambers, casting Brontes's silhouette across the stone floor. He stood tall with his muscular arms crossed over his chest. His shirtless frame highlighted the broadness of his shoulders and the chiseled lines of his chest.

"Did you now?" He smiled, and his navy eyes gleamed with a mixture of amusement and adoration as his hand brushed over the stubble dusting his defined jawline.

"Come see." I stepped aside to let him peer through the telescope. As he did, our hands found each other naturally, intertwining like two vines reaching for the same sun.

With his free hand, he adjusted the telescope slightly, marveling at the dazzling constellation I'd been observing. I leaned into his side, relishing his natural warmth.

Brontes hummed, his chest vibrating against me. "It's beautiful, though not nearly as radiant as you."

"Flatterer." I playfully pushed his bare chest, my fingertips tingling at the contact with his skin, and sighed. "You know, stargazing always makes me feel part of something grand and infinite."

Brontes drew me close, nuzzling the curve of my neck. A soft sigh escaped me as his lips traveled up to my ear, his warm breath fanning over my skin. "I know of other ways to make you see stars."

Though my heartbeat quickened at his suggestive tone and the simmering desire in his gaze, I wouldn't give in that easily.

"Is that a challenge, Your Majesty?" I teased, raising an eyebrow in mock defiance. "I doubt you could even make me see a single star."

"Really, Your Highness?" His eyes danced with mischief as they locked onto mine. "Brave words for a princess who claims to be shy."

Our lips were now inches apart, the magnetic pull between us growing stronger with each passing moment.

"Show me then, Storm King," I breathed. A newfound boldness surged through me. The night air hummed with electric anticipation. "I'm still waiting."

My head tilted up to meet his lips in a slow, deep kiss that stole my breath away. Our tongues danced and dueled, igniting our passion like a storm raging along the serene celestial canvas above.

"See stars yet?" Brontes whispered against my lips, a playful smile tugging at the corners of his mouth.

"Maybe half a star," I replied as I pressed myself tighter against him. "But I'm sure you can do better."

"Challenge accepted," he grumbled before capturing my lips once more in a searing kiss as fiery as a thousand burning suns.

As our mouths explored one another, my hands ran through his tousled black hair, our breaths mingling in the heated space between us. Brontes's arms wrapped around me, pulling me impossibly closer, our bodies pressed together like two puzzle pieces finally finding their match.

He walked me backward until I felt the solid surface of the wall behind me. He caged me in, one hand on either side of my head as he devoured my lips.

I parted my legs, hooking one around his hip to draw him closer. The hard length of his arousal pressed into the cradle of my thighs, eliciting a throaty groan from him.

Brontes trailed hot, open-mouthed kisses along my jaw and down my neck, grazing his teeth over my pulse point. I shuddered, tangling my hands in his hair to hold him there.

"So beautiful," he rasped against my skin. "All mine." His hand slid under my gown, fingers dancing over my inner thigh.

Heat coiled low in my belly at his words, my body awakening to his skillful touch. I whimpered softly, desire and need clouding my thoughts until only one remained.

My Brontes.

A low growl rumbled in his chest as he crushed his mouth to mine once more. Our kisses turned frantic, hands roving and grasping. Brontes's fingers hooked underneath the straps of my gown and pulled them down over my arms. His eyes intensely watched as my breasts spilled out.

"You are so exquisite," he said, his chest heaving as he raked his gaze over my flesh.

His fingers trailed reverently over my flushed skin before palming my breast and rolling my nipple between his fingers until it pebbled.

When I whimpered at his touch, he growled softly, leaning down to capture a nipple between his teeth. He tugged it into his hot mouth, flicking his tongue over the hard peak.

The feel of his rough stubble against my tender skin sent a bolt of pleasure straight to my core. I writhed against him, my hands clutching his shoulders as I tried to pull him in tighter.

The hand that wasn't busy tormenting my breast trailed down my body, his fingers following the curve of my abdomen until he reached the juncture between my hip and thigh. My breath hitched when his fingers danced along the edge of my panties, pressing down against the aching flesh between my thighs.

Molten waves of pleasure pulsed through me, settling in my core as his fingers dipped into the wet heat between my thighs. I cried out when his fingers stroked over my swollen, sensitive nub, his thumb sliding over it in a slow, maddening circle.

My body soaked for him as need coiled hot and tight within me, an aching void only Brontes could fill. I fumbled with the laces of his pajama pants, shoving the offending garment down his hips. His arousal sprang free, hard and ready.

I took him in my hand, delighting in the strangled groan that escaped him. He pushed into my fist, and I mewed as he continued to pleasure me.

"Tell me what you want, Princess," he commanded in my ear, his breath hot and heavy against my skin.

"I want all of you, my king," I whispered breathlessly.

"That's it," he growled, stilling my movements. "I'm going to bury myself deep inside you."

I gasped softly, and my heart stuttered at his words.

Brontes swept me off my feet and cradled me in his taut arms. He carried me to the large round daybed on the terrace, gently setting me down on the plush pillows and soft blankets that adorned it. As he lowered himself over me, I lost myself in the lustful glint in his dark eyes. The warmth of his skin against mine sent sparks of electricity cascading through my very being, only making me long for more of him.

I wanted to feel him everywhere. I wanted him inside me so that I could be a part of him . . . be one with him.

He was my soulmate. He was my everything.

I wanted to be his queen.

I wanted to be his wife.

I wanted to be the mother of his children.

"I love you, Gwyneira," he whispered, as if he could read my thoughts.

"I love you, Brontes." I smiled at him lovingly.

His hands dipped under my gown again, pushing the sheer fabric up around my waist and sliding my panties off. His eyes burned red hot as they traveled across my nakedness.

He nudged my legs apart, settling himself between them, and my breath hitched as his tip brushed my entrance. With one vigorous thrust, he drove into me, filling me so deliciously that I cried out, certain I would shatter.

"Gwyneira," he groaned and stilled to rain kisses down my neck, my throat, my chest.

"Brontes," I begged, my voice breathless.

"You want more?" he asked huskily.

"Yes," I whimpered.

He abruptly pulled out and thrusted into me again. "Like that?"

"Yes . . . please . . ." I gasped.

His firm, broad chest caressed my breasts as he leaned over, thrusting into me again and again. My body began to quake as the delightful fire in my core threatened to claim me.

"I'm so close." I arched my back into him. "Give me all of you."

With one final powerful thrust and a loud groan, he pulsated against my walls, releasing his essence into me. The waves of ecstasy crashed over me, sending me over the edge. I cried out. My nails dug into his scarred back as I clung to him, shuddering as the most incredible, most intense sensation ripped through me.

He held himself there for a moment, buried deep inside me as he had promised. Finally, he collapsed on top of me, his strong body relaxing as he tucked his head into my neck.

"Gwyneira," he whispered as he kissed my neck. "My beautiful snowflake."

"My Brontes." I snuggled into him. "My love. My king."

In the afterglow, his arms remained securely around me, unwilling to let go just yet. We lay tangled together under the dazzling vastness of the night sky, the only witness to our act of passion.

"Oh no!" I sat up suddenly, reaching to pull my nightgown back over my exposed body.

Brontes's head popped up with alarm. "What is it?"

"I forgot we were outside! I hope no one heard us." The heat of embarrassment rushed to my cheeks at the thought.

"Too late now, Princess!" Brontes laughed as he rose from the daybed. "But let's go inside before we fall asleep out here."

Once again, Brontes scooped me up into his large, firm arms. With the cloud of desire lifted, I savored his scent of cedarwood and musk and the safety I felt in his grasp, like nothing could ever harm me.

Brontes smiled down, his eyes now full of love and tenderness, as he carried me into our bedroom.

The sun peeked through the towering windows of the Storm Castle's halls, casting a warm golden glow on the marble floors and intricate tapestries. Brontes walked beside me, his strong arm wrapped protectively around my waist as we made our way to the royal dining hall for breakfast.

"Has there been any response from Fannar?" I asked, unable to mask the hope in my voice.

Brontes shook his head. "Nothing yet."

My shoulders slumped as I let out a small sigh. I hadn't received a response to any of my letters to Fannar, not even the one I'd sent on my last day in the Ice Kingdom. Worry knotted in my stomach, but I quickly pushed it down. "He must be busy with his studies at Haven Academy," I said out loud, allowing the words to comfort my thoughts.

Noticing my crestfallen expression, Brontes placed a reassuring hand on my arm. "Why don't you go visit him at the academy? I know you miss him."

I leaned into his warm touch. As much as I ached to see Fannar, the thought of leaving Brontes twisted my insides. "Not when you need me here. You're still establishing your cabinet of royal advisors. I want to be here to support you."

Brontes started to protest, but I silenced him with a finger to his lips. "We'll go to him together once your cabinet is settled." I offered him a small smile. "I want the two of you to meet properly and, hopefully, before our actual wedding day!"

Brontes chuckled, the sound rumbling through his broad chest. "Fine. There's no arguing with you, my queen." His fingers tightened around my waist, pulling me closer to him. "We'll both go find Fannar. I promise." He planted a soft kiss on my cheek as we approached the dining room.

A deafening crash shattered the moment. We jerked apart, pulses racing. Another resounding boom, closer now. The acrid scent of smoke seared my nostrils. Brontes instinctively pulled me into him, and we exchanged alarmed glances as bangs echoed down the hall.

"Wh-what was that?" I stuttered, my heart pounding in my chest.

"I don't know." Brontes stepped between me and the sounds. His hands flared with electricity, ready for whatever might be the source of the commotion.

"Did your parents escape the dungeon?"

"I don't think so. The noise isn't coming from underground."

Before we could take another step, the intensity of the crashes increased, accompanied by the unmistakable sounds of fighting. The clamor was drawing nearer. I held my breath with anticipation.

"Your Majesties!" A guard barreled around the corner, his stoic face etched with determination. "The castle is under attack! We must get you to the underground bunker immediately!"

"Under attack?" Brontes's eyes darkened with fury. "We must defend the castle! I won't abandon my people!"

Cid, the captain of the king's guard, arrived with additional soldiers. "Your Majesty, I insist you go to the bunker for your own protection. You cannot help the people if you are captured or killed."

"I won't hide like a coward!" Brontes retorted.

"Please, Your Majesty," Cid implored. "Think of the Princess."

Brontes looked at me with conflicted concern. He hesitated for a moment, then nodded, his jaw clenched. "Alright. But only until the Princess is safe."

Cid nodded in agreement. As we followed the guards toward the bunker, Brontes gripped my hand tightly as we ran amidst the chaos, determination steeling his jaw. But I saw the fear in his eyes—fear for my safety. The crashes seemed to stalk us, growing louder and more fearsome with every step we took.

Just as we were about to reach the bunker, a tremendous force threw me from Brontes's side. I crashed to the floor, dazed. Brontes slammed into the opposite wall, while the guards flew backward, away from both of us.

My vision blurred, and a wave of horror washed over me like a torrential storm. We were under siege, the castle breached. The walls shuddered, rippling and buckling inward until they finally exploded in a shower of fire and smoke. The debris scattered everywhere, large chunks of stone and mortar hurled in all directions as bright, hissing flames engulfed the hallway, separating us from the guards.

I scrambled to my feet, panic rising. Brontes was already up, his eyes and hands wild with sparks, rushing to put himself between me and the impending danger.

"Brontes!" I screamed, reaching out for him. The ground beneath us shook again, making it nearly impossible to keep my balance.

"Gwyneira, get to the bunker!" he bellowed back at me.

I hesitated. From his stance, it was clear he had no intention of seeking refuge inside the bunker. Fighting was his only plan. My home had become a cacophony of destruction, but every instinct screamed at me to stay with him.

A stray ball of fire sizzled past my head, scorching the wall behind me. I gasped, my head snapping to face the broken wall where the fireball had emerged. Surely, our attacker was a Fire Enchanted. The Fire Kingdom accused the Ice Kingdom of murdering their princess years ago.

Had they come to take their revenge by slaying me, the Ice Kingdom's only princess?

Brontes raised his arms up, deflecting a barrage of icy spikes with a shield of wind. My heart stuttered. *Ice Enchanted?*

As I stumbled back, trying to process what was happening, a figure suddenly shot out from behind the fiery wall and darted to Brontes, slugging him across the face.

"No!" I screamed. Icicles formed in my hands as I prepared to defend my home.

And then, through the haze of smoke, confusion, and fear, I saw him. I almost didn't recognize him dressed in all black.

Fannar?

My beloved older brother stood tall and formidable, his shoulder-length white hair whipping around his face like a tempest, glacial blue eyes cold and unyielding, his hands glowing with icy power. He looked every bit the powerful prince he was, but there was a darkness I had never seen before. *What is Fannar doing here with a Fire Enchanted?*

Fannar unleashed another torrent of icy spears at Brontes. I barely recognized the vengeful figure before me as the same person who had once snuck books and candy to my room. He was now locked in a life-or-death battle with my fiancé.

Brontes roared, unleashing a thunderclap. Fannar countered it easily, icy fractals spiraling from his palms. They clashed again and again, neither gaining ground.

"Run, Gwyneira! Get to the bunker!" Brontes yelled, dodging Fannar's relentless attacks.

My body trembled, paralyzed by my swirling emotions, unable to tear my eyes away. Every fiber of my being was being torn apart, watching the two most important people in my life fight one another. Ice and lightning clashed around them, illuminating their equally matched power and heightening the intensity of their battle.

The sheer force of Fannar's ice powers sent Brontes hurling toward the wall, freezing him in place. In response, Brontes unleashed a tornado that tore through the castle corridor, its deafening roar filling my ears.

Suddenly, a hand clamped down on my arm. I cried out as fingers seared my skin, and I looked up at a beautiful but tough-looking girl with flame-red hair also dressed in all black. Her piercing emerald-green eyes bore into mine with a determination that mirrored Fannar's.

"Got her!" she shouted to my brother. "Let's go!"

Fannar's eyes flicked up, and he rushed behind my captor. I struggled to pull my arm out of the girl's fiery grasp, but she tightened her hold on me, burning into me like a brand as she started to drag me away. I yelped in pain.

"*NO, GWYNEIRA!*" Brontes roared in desperation, his eyes wild with anger and helplessness. His anguished shout shattered my heart.

The sight of me being dragged away gave Brontes a second wind. His muscles strained against the icy bonds that held him to the wall, and, heaving with tremendous effort, he managed to break free, sending chunks of frost flying in every direction.

He charged forward, slamming his enormous body into Fannar with a loud thud. The two men crashed to the ground in a flurry of fists and ice shards. Despite Brontes's larger size and greater strength, Fannar coated himself in a slippery layer of ice that made it difficult for Brontes to grapple him. Resolve crystallized within me. This needed to stop.

"BOTH OF YOU, STOP!" I yelled, finally finding my voice. Ice and lightning burst from my body, forcing the Fire Enchanted to release me in a shock of pain.

I stumbled forward, catching myself before falling to the ground. Brontes lunged toward me, but Fannar stepped in front of him, both looking ready to continue their fight.

"Fannar, what are you doing?!" I shouted, my chest heaving with frustration. "Brontes, put him down!"

"Fannar? Your brother?" Brontes held him by the collar and looked down at him in confusion.

"And who are you?" I demanded, turning to the fire girl.

Fannar and the girl looked at each other, but before anyone could answer, a swirling vortex of dark blues and purples sliced through the air, appearing before us. The portal, speckled with what seemed like tiny shimmering stars, crackled with energy, making every hair on my body stand on end.

Out of the portal stepped a woman unlike anyone I had ever seen. She looked to be a few years older than Brontes, with long, dark brown hair that flowed down her back, contrasting against her pale skin and eerily yellow eyes. She stood tall and regal, her mysterious aura enhanced by the futuristic clothing she wore. Sleek black garments hugged her body tightly, adorned with shimmering silver accents that resembled the night sky.

The mysterious woman's gaze fell on Brontes and Fannar. Brontes had Fannar by the collar, both of their faces bloody and battered from fighting with each other. Her lips curved into a sinister smile.

"Yes, finally!" she cackled with wicked laughter.

The four of us froze in place, staring blankly at the woman in black.

The Fire Enchanted let me go and stormed a few steps toward her. "Who the hell are you, lady?!"

With a casual flick of her wrist, the mysterious woman sent the fire girl soaring through the air.

"Helena!" Fannar screamed.

Helena. My brother's anxious tone made it clear he cared for this girl. My mind raced, trying to piece together how he would be connected to this Fire Enchanted.

Then, my heart shuddered as the strange woman approached Brontes with a wide, sick smile.

"Now, my beloved Storm Prince—kill him!"

Beloved Storm Prince?!

"What?" Brontes asked with as much confusion as I felt.

"Kill the Ice Prince!" she sneered. "And we can begin our reign of terror!"

CHAPTER TWO

HELENA

The plan had been to sneak into the Storm Castle and sneak back out with Fannar's sister without anyone noticing.

The royal guards spotted us almost immediately once we set foot in the castle. When the fighting started, we knocked down walls, drawing even more unwanted attention. Then, it turned out Gwyneira was not as powerless nor defenseless as Fannar remembered, fighting me tooth and nail as I tried to help her escape.

Needless to say, our rescue mission wasn't going according to plan. Now, this crazy woman had showed up and blasted me halfway across the room.

Headmaster Moira was the only Cosmic Enchanted I'd ever seen in my life, but from the brief glimpse I'd gotten of this woman's powers, it was obvious she was a Cosmic Enchanted.

As I pulled myself off the floor, she fixed her gaze onto Brontes, the yellow flecks in her eyes shimmering with a dangerous, menacing glint. Her lips curved upward into a wolfish smile.

"Kill him," she hissed again. "Kill Fannar, and we can rule the Enchanted Realm together!"

I breathed a short sigh of relief as Brontes let go of Fannar before his face twisted into a snarl, his dark eyes flashing with rage. "I'm not killing anyone for you. Who the hell do you think you are, and why are you in my castle?"

The woman tilted her head back and laughed with a chilling cackle that made me cringe. "Oh, my love. I'm Obsidia, the future queen of the Enchanted Realm and the love of your life! Or I was in my dimension."

Say what now?

She stepped closer to him, running a finger down his chest like a creepy stalker. "Together, we conquered all the kingdoms and ruled the entire realm as its king and queen. With the power of dark magic, we destroyed anyone who dared to oppose us, and now it's time to do it again, my love!"

Brontes shoved her hand away, disgust plain on his face. "You're insane. I would never try to conquer the Enchanted Realm, let alone rule with you. I'd die first."

"But darling, we're meant to be together," Obsidia pouted. "Don't you feel our bond?"

Brontes scoffed. "The only bond I feel is with Gwyneira."

Obsidia paused and fixed her gaze on Gwyneira. "Ugh, the Ice Princess. Well, that explains it." She clicked her tongue disapprovingly. "That damn prophecy. Every timeline where you meet her, you never reach your full potential."

"What are you talking about?" Brontes demanded.

"You were magnificent back then. Overwhelmed with power. I've never seen anything like it again. Your rage unleased the fearsome monster within you! It was so beautiful." She reached for him, but he leaned away from her in disgust. "It all starts in this moment, Brontes. Kill the Ice Prince, and we can be together."

Brontes reached down, and I summoned fire to my hands, thinking he might try to hurt Fannar. Instead, he grabbed Fannar's hand and helped him to his feet.

"I would never kill Gwyneira's brother, especially not to be with you," Brontes grumbled. "I love Gwyneira. I don't even know you!"

"But I know *you*," Obsidia countered.

"No, you don't. You know who I would've been if I hadn't met Gwyneira. I'm not that man, and I never will be."

"You are!" she insisted, angry desperation leaking into her voice. "You just don't realize how great you could be!"

A little guilt passed over his eyes. "You're wrong. I do know . . . The all-consuming power, the rage you're talking about . . . but that's not me, thanks to Gwyneira." He looked at Fannar's sister lovingly before his eyes darted sharply toward Obsidia again. "I *never* want to be that man again!"

This time, Obsidia's eerie yellow eyes narrowed with rage at Gwyneira. "This is your fault, little mouse!"

"Leave her out of this," Brontes growled, his hands sparking with lightning.

"Ah, but if I kill her, the prophecy will never be fulfilled," Obsidia purred, raising her hand as dark purple energy crackled between her fingers. "You'll become the notorious Storm Prince I know, and then you'll be mine again!"

The room crackled with energy, dark tendrils of Obsidia's magic coiling and lashing out like serpents toward Gwyneira, who still stood beside me.

"Watch out!" I yelled, rushing forward. Fire burst from my fingertips, meeting the black magic midair and enveloping it in a burst of flames.

"Gwyneira!" Icicles shot from Fannar's hands at the sorceress attacking his sister.

Brontes was right beside him, lightning arcing between his fingers as he hurled bolts at Obsidia.

"Stay back, Gwyneira," I warned, grabbing her arm as she tried to step into the fray.

"But I can help!" Gwyneira protested with determination. "I won't let her hurt Brontes or Fannar!"

"No, it's you that she wants. It's too risky," I insisted, looking straight into her icy blue eyes to emphasize my request. "We can handle this. Just stay safe."

After Gwyneira relented and backed further away, I rejoined the boys in the fight.

"Your attempts to stop me are pathetic," Obsidia sneered, dodging Fannar's ice and Brontes's lightning with ease. "You'll never defeat me."

Fannar growled, launching another volley of icicles at her.

"Give up, Obsidia." Brontes's voice strained as he conjured a tornado. "You're outnumbered and outmatched!"

"Never, not until the Ice Princess is dead!" she spat, raising her hands to unleash more dark magic.

"That's not happening, you witch!" I shouted, shielding the guys from Obsidia's attack with a wall of fire. The darkness flickered and died against the flames, but stopping that one attack was enough to strain my powers.

"Enough!" Fannar roared, summoning a massive deluge of ice that surged toward Obsidia.

Brontes grunted loudly, his storm powers amplifying the ice into deadly bullets of hail. The onslaught forced Obsidia back, her face contorted with fury and pain.

"Helena, now!" Fannar urged.

I gritted my teeth, sweat beading on my brow as I mustered my remaining energy into one final attack. I screamed, sending a firestorm blazing toward Obsidia, the heat so intense it threatened to consume everything in its path.

"Ahhhh!" she cried out, throwing up a dark barrier to protect herself from the combined force of our powers, but even her formidable defenses wouldn't hold up long.

A dark purple and black portal formed behind her.

"Get out of my castle!" Brontes growled.

"Ugh!" she sneered, her yellow eyes glowing with hatred. "This isn't the last you'll see of me." Obsidia turned to Gwyneira. "When we meet again, you will die, little mouse."

"Over our dead bodies!" Fannar declared, his powers shimmering around him like icy armor.

"Oh, dear Ice Prince, it will be." Obsidia stared us down with fierce intensity, her eyes blazing with anger. "I'll be even more powerful. You, your precious sister, and your

Fire Princess will all die by my hand. And Brontes, my love, you will be mine again." She looked at Brontes one more time as she retreated into the portal. "Until we meet again, my king!"

And with that, the portal vanished in a burst of darkness, leaving nothing but an eerie silence in its wake.

"Brontes!" Gwyneira cried and ran into his arms.

Ash and a few small cuts littered the Storm Prince's tanned face, and dust from the fallen stone walls speckled his long, wavy black hair. But none of that mattered. His dark eyes brightened as soon as he heard his name leave Gwyneira's lips. He opened his arms wide and cocooned her in a fierce embrace. Brontes was an intimidatingly large man, and Gwyneira appeared so small compared to him, much younger than eighteen. Her delicate features gave her an aura of ethereal innocence.

Brontes held her protectively as he stroked her long white hair and kissed her forehead.

"Are you alright, snowflake?" he asked Gwyneira gently, cupping her face in his hands.

She nodded, wiping away tears from her eyes with trembling fingers. "I-I'm fine," she said softly. "What about you? I was so frightened for you and Fannar." She snuggled into his chest.

Hmmm . . . Gwyneira certainly didn't look like she needed rescuing.

I waved my hand to extinguish the remaining smoldering fires around us, and my knees buckled underneath me, exhaustion taking hold as the adrenaline faded.

"Helena!" Fannar rushed to my side, concern cracking his normally passive expression as his eyes met mine. "Helena, are you alright?"

"Never better." I forced a smile. "Just tired." I touched Fannar's swollen face. "Are you okay? You took quite a pummeling from the Storm Prince."

Fannar smirked. "You should see the other guy."

"Funny." I smirked back.

Gwyneira looked over at me and Fannar hesitantly, Brontes's arms still wrapped around her. "Thank you for protecting me, Helena."

"Anytime." I smiled genuinely this time.

"Your Majesty!" a voice shouted.

The hallway was now clear of smoke and flames, allowing the royal guards to take their positions around us. They had their swords raised and ready to protect their prince.

Brontes held up his hand and waved them off. "Stand down," he said. "The enemy is gone."

"But what about these intruders?" the captain questioned, glaring at Fannar and me.

"He's my brother," Gwyneira replied.

The guards hesitated before sheathing their swords and bowing in respect.

Then, Brontes's eyebrows knitted in a scowl. "Though . . . why *did* you attack us in my castle?"

"Not yet, Brontes." Gwyneira touched his chest to calm him. "I think proper introductions are in order first." She gestured dramatically toward Fannar. "Your Majesty, this is my older brother, His Royal Highness Fannar, Crown Prince of the Ice Kingdom." And then, she looked at Fannar but gestured with a curtesy to Brontes. "Fannar, this is my fiancé, His Majesty Brontes, King of the Storm Kingdom."

"Your Majesty." Fannar bowed his head in reverence.

"King?!" I unintentionally exclaimed out loud.

"Yes, we staged a coup against his parents, so Brontes is king now," Gwyneira continued. "I told you in my letter, Fannar."

"No, your letter begged me to come save you because you didn't want to marry a monster," Fannar expressed confusion and a tinge of frustration. "That's why we came to rescue you."

Brontes stiffened, frowning. “I apologize for the kidnapping of your sister. It was my parents’ doing, and I had no say in it.”

“Technically, it was an arranged marriage her parents agreed to, so it wasn’t *really* a kidnapping,” I pointed out, but no one cared.

“You’ve apologized enough, my love,” Gwyneira stopped him. “If our marriage hadn’t been arranged, we wouldn’t have found each other.” She clasped Brontes’s hand adoringly and turned to Fannar. “I got to know Brontes, and we fell in love. I sent you another letter. I guess you didn’t get that one, brother?”

Fannar’s expression didn’t change, but his eyes softened ever so slightly as he shook his head.

“I invited you to come to the Storm Castle so you could properly meet Brontes,” she giggled at the irony. “I wrote about how amazing he is and how we’d decided to get married by our own choice.”

Her cheeks glowed and her eyes sparkled as she spoke so sweetly about him. She clasped her hands together in delight, and a smile never left her face.

“That’s wonderful, Gwyneira!” I smiled. When Fannar didn’t say anything, I elbowed him. “It’s that wonderful, Fannar? Your sister is happy here.”

"Yes, that's great," Fannar managed to say. "I'm just glad you're okay."

I cleared my throat so Fannar would look at me.

"Oh, sorry," he said. "This is my girlfriend, Helena. We met at the academy."

"You're a Fire Enchanted?" Gwyneira asked and stared at Fannar in disbelief. "I thought interacting with Fire Enchanted was forbidden, let alone dating one."

"It was," Fannar nodded. "Our parents tried to kill her, though they won't admit it. But they've accepted her now."

"Are you serious?!" Gwyneira's eyes looked like they might fall out of their sockets.

"Yes, she's even staying at the Ice Castle during winter break."

"And you're the Fire Princess?" Brontes asked.

"Nope." I shook my head, finally piping up. "Just a lowly commoner among all you royals."

"But Obsidia called you the Fire Princess," Brontes recalled.

"She did," Gwyneira agreed.

I shrugged. "She must've mistaken me for someone else."

Fannar thought for a moment. "I heard Headmaster Moira say the lost princess of the Fire Kingdom was found at another academy."

"Hmmm . . . Perhaps Obsidia confused you for her?" Brontes pondered.

"Probably. I've never been to the Fire Kingdom. I'm from the Unenchanted Realm."

"Really?" Gwyneira gasped. "You have to tell me all about it!"

"Sure." I chuckled. "As long as you tell me how you have both ice and storm powers!"

Gwyneira giggled with excitement. "Brontes and I are Combined Enchanted!"

"Though I haven't found my ice powers yet," Brontes added.

Fannar and I looked at each other. "We're also Combined Enchanted," he said hesitantly. "But we don't have any other powers yet either."

"And you thought your baby sister was defenseless." I jabbed Fannar. "She's got more powers than any of us!"

Gwyneira beamed proudly.

An awkward silence fell over us as we looked around at the damage. Fannar and I had caused so much destruction in our attempt to rescue Gwyneira, even before Obsidia showed up. I glanced at him sheepishly.

"Your Majesty," Fannar said, looking Brontes straight in the eyes with a sincere expression on his face. "I apologize for the damage to your castle. I understand if you're angry with us."

"Please call me Brontes," he replied as he shook his head and smiled sadly. "No apology necessary. I understand that you were trying to save Gwyneira. Trust me, if I believed she was in danger, I would have leveled this place to the ground." He glanced at her before turning back to us with a wry smile on his face. "But please don't destroy my castle again," he joked, his eyes twinkling with amusement.

Gwyneira giggled. "Don't worry, they won't!" She finally threw her arms around Fannar, embracing him in a tight hug. Tears glimmered in her eyes as she whispered, "I missed you so much, brother."

He hugged her back. "I missed you too, sister. I was so worried about you, but I'm glad you are happy here."

I glanced at Brontes, who wore a wide grin that must have matched mine at sight of the siblings' sweet reunion.

"Please at least let us make the repairs," I offered.

Brontes shook his head. "No need. I've got some great contractors for that."

"They made me an observatory twice!" Gwyneira exclaimed.

"An observatory?" Fannar's face perked up with curiosity.

"Yes! You must see it, brother. Now that you're here, you must stay for a few days!"

"Yes, you must stay," Brontes agreed. "Obsidia said she'll be back, and we need to spend time figuring out what to do . . . for Gwyneira's safety, at the very least."

Fannar and I exchanged glances, and I shrugged. I knew Fannar couldn't argue with that.

"Okay." Fannar nodded. "We'll stay to plan our strategy for dealing with Obsidia."

Gwyneira jumped up and down excitedly as she grabbed each of us by the arm and began dragging us toward the dining room. "First, we'll have breakfast, and then you have to see my observatory!"

Brontes, Fannar, and I all chuckled at her enthusiasm.

CHAPTER THREE
GWYNEIRA

The past three days had been a whirlwind of exploring, eating, and bonding that I'd never expected. Brontes and I gave Helena and Fannar the grand tour of the castle, introduced them to all my friends on the castle staff, and shared so many laughs. Growing up, I had rarely shared meals with Fannar, so being able to share our favorite foods together with Brontes and Helena in the royal dining room meant so much to me. It felt like we were truly a family now, even though much had changed since I had last seen my brother.

Fannar had always been protective, but there was a new strength in him, fueled by his love for Helena. It warmed my heart to see how he allowed himself to be vulnerable around her, revealing a tender side I hadn't seen in years.

My initial hesitation about Helena still lingered at the back of my mind. After all, the Fire and Ice Kingdoms' rift was generations old. But watching her now, I couldn't help but admire her autumnal beauty. Her presence was like a warm hearth on a cold winter's night, drawing everyone near. Despite her feisty and blunt nature, she spoke with confidence and authority that commanded respect. I envied her, especially since everyone around me treated me as if I were fragile and in need of protection, despite having both ice and storm powers.

My gaze swept through Brontes's study. Brontes stood with his back to the immense stone fireplace, arms crossed over his broad chest. Tongues of flame cast flickering shadows over his handsome, brooding features.

Fannar leaned against the far wall beneath an arched window, silvery moonlight glinting off his white hair. Though he held himself with typical aloofness, tension radiated from his eyes.

Helena perched on the edge of the huge map table in the center of the room, her casual posture belying the anticipation etched on her face. Firelight danced across her cinnamon locks as she bounced her leg restlessly.

I found myself drawn to the cozy window seat nestled beside a bookcase, needing the comfort of my favorite reading nook. Outside, the inky night sky foretold the coming storm as the first rumbles of thunder echoed across the kingdom.

"She'll be back," Brontes said bluntly, cutting through the silence in the room. "Obsidia has made her intentions clear. She wants Gwyneira and Fannar dead."

I shuddered, the memory of our last terrifying encounter with the rogue Cosmic Enchanted still fresh in my mind. Helena placed a comforting hand on my arm, her expression unusually solemn.

"We'll just have to be ready for her next time," she said with a confident resolve.

Fannar nodded, his jaw clenched tight beneath stone cold eyes. "But we need allies. The four of us alone won't be enough, not against the kind of power she wields."

"You're right," Brontes agreed.

"Which kingdoms are you on good terms with?" Helena asked.

I glanced at Brontes nervously. "We only have an official alliance with the Ice Kingdom from our arranged marriage."

"But we're not on *bad* terms with any kingdom," Brontes added.

"Though the Fire Kingdom probably won't help since they are still feuding with the Ice Kingdom." Fannar frowned.

"Who does that leave?" Helena asked.

"Water, Earth, and Air," I replied.

"But Water and Earth also hate each other," Fannar said.

"Are you serious?!" Helena exclaimed. "What is wrong with you Enchanted people?"

"Hundreds of years of bitter history." Brontes sighed. "We need help from whomever we can get, so I'll send envoys to the Earth, Water, and Air Kingdoms requesting their aid. We'll just have to see who agrees."

"We need to anticipate Obsidia's next move," Fannar said, breaking the pensive silence. "Where is she likely to appear next?"

Helena drummed her fingers on the table anxiously. "I mean, she said she was going to be back, so I assumed she meant here at the Storm Castle."

Brontes growled as he began pacing again, his heavy boots echoing in the stone room with each step. "We've already done a lot to strengthen our defenses and increase security. All guards and staff members will continue to receive extra training in their powers every day."

I spoke up tentatively. "What if we tried luring her into a trap somehow? We could lay false leads to bait her."

Fannar nodded thoughtfully. "Hmmm . . . That's an interesting strategy. Perhaps a decoy?"

"Ooh, I like that idea!" Helena said. "We could catch her off guard."

I chewed my lip pensively. "It might help if we knew more about Obsidia's weaknesses. Everyone has a weakness, even someone as powerful as a Cosmic Enchanted."

"Yeah, about that!" Helena jumped off the table suddenly. "How is there another Cosmic Enchanted? I thought Headmaster Moira was the only one?"

"Headmaster Moira?" I asked.

"Our headmaster at Haven Academy," Fannar explained to me. "And yes, that is what I thought too."

Brontes nodded. "Your headmaster was the only Cosmic Enchanted I'd ever heard of."

"Do you think she know about Obsidia?" Helena asked.

"No idea." Fannar shrugged.

"Hmmmm," I pondered. "If Cosmic Enchanted can travel through time and space, there is really no way of knowing how many there might be across all timelines and realities."

"True," Fannar said. "I guess the only person who would have any idea is Headmaster Moira herself."

"It sounds like you two should go back to Haven Academy," I suggested. "Since Headmaster Moira is the only known Cosmic Enchanted, she can give us some insight on Obsidia, or at least her possible weaknesses."

"Good idea, sister," Fannar agreed, nodding thoughtfully. "But we need to return to the Ice Kingdom first. Our parents expect us back, and I don't want them to worry."

"Of course," Helena added, her hand squeezing Fannar's for reassurance. "We can head back to the Ice Kingdom tomorrow morning and let your parents know what's happening. Then, we can go back to the academy to talk to Headmaster Moira."

"What about dark magic?" I asked. "Obsidia said that the power of dark magic helped her conquer the other realms."

"Yes, I've heard of dark magic sorcerers during my history lessons with Father but not much," Brontes answered. "As far as we knew, they've been banished from the Enchanted Realm for a long time."

"Well, they might not be gone for long." Helena grimaced at Fannar. "We should do some research on them at the academy library."

Fannar nodded in agreement. "And ask Headmaster Moira if she knows anything about them too."

"In the meantime, I'll see what I can find about dark magic in the castle library," I offered. "Nana Osborne used to dust the books, and she said we should have some texts about it."

Brontes nodded. "It's not much, but it's a start."

"Are you sure she'll be safe here?" Fannar asked Brontes, though his eyes were squarely on me.

"Always," Brontes promised, his hand resting on my shoulder. "If I can't be with her, she'll have multiple guards protecting her."

My jaw tightened and my fist clenched. I stood a little straighter at their overprotectiveness. I possessed more powers than they did, yet their words sounded as if I was a child that needed to be watched over. As if I wasn't right there with them.

"I can take care of myself, you know," I muttered, failing to suppress my annoyance.

"Of course, you can!" Helena chimed in with a cheery, supportive grin. "But we all need to look out for each other."

"Absolutely." Fannar gave me a small, apologetic smile. "We need *everyone* to stay safe."

"Fine," I conceded quietly.

"Okay, it's settled," Fannar concluded. "Helena and I will return to the Ice Kingdom tomorrow morning and explain the situation to my parents. Then, we'll go to Haven Academy to ask Headmaster Moira about Obsidia."

Helena and I nodded.

"And you'll call us as soon as you find anything?" Brontes asked.

"Of cour—" Fannar began.

"Wait, call?" Helena interrupted. "You mean you and Gwyneira could've called each other this whole time?! What's with all the snail mail letters then?!"

Brontes, Fannar, and I shared glances at each other.

"I wasn't going to call the Storm Castle," Fannar stated. "I thought Gwyneira was being held against her will! They weren't going to let me speak to her."

"And I didn't call the Ice Castle because our parents would've never let me talk to Fannar," I explained. "They would've hung up the second they realized it was me."

Brontes nodded along.

Helena sighed with exasperation. "Man, you Enchanted people make everything so damn complicated."

I giggled first, followed by Fannar and Brontes breaking into laughter. It filled the room, lightening the unbearably tense atmosphere.

"I don't think it's funny," Helena huffed.

"It's okay, babe." Fannar's eyes lit up as he gazed at her. The corners of his mouth curved into the most loving, endearing smile I'd ever seen on his face, and it made my heart swell with joy.

"Why don't we start packing?" Fannar suggested.

"Good idea," Brontes said. "Then, we can enjoy a farewell dinner together tonight, and you two can get some rest."

"Sounds good," Helena remarked. "We'll see ya later."

As I watched Fannar and Helena leave hand in hand, a pang of sadness squeezed my heart. We had only spent a couple of days together. Who knew when I'd see him again? He probably would be busy once school started back at Haven Academy.

I tried to push those thoughts away for now.

"Hey," Brontes said gently, embracing my shoulders from behind. "You're already thinking about missing Fannar again, aren't you?"

I smiled as I saw the knowing look in his eyes, despite the lifetime I'd spent learning to suppress my emotions.

"He's not going yet, my snowflake, so don't get sad until he's actually gone, okay?"

"Okay." I lightly grasped his heavy forearms.

The previous conversations about our strategy and planning replayed in my mind. Despite the circumstances, it was nice to feel like I was part of a team, my input valued just as highly as my brother's or Brontes's.

"Want to see if Maisol has any cookies for us to munch on?" Brontes asked slyly.

"We're going to eat dinner soon!" I rebutted.

"Eh, it's just a snack. Come on." He pulled me to my feet.

I giggled, and we headed to the kitchen in search of cookies.

CHAPTER FOUR
HELENA

As it came into view, the frosty landscape of the Ice Castle shimmered in the sunlight, and a blanket of snow draped over the sprawling grounds. Our carriage clattered as its wheels crunched against the frozen earth, and the clop of unicorn hooves echoed against the walls of the courtyard.

The four ice unicorns pulling our carriage had long silver horns on their heads, sparkling in the light of the winter sun. Their thick, ivory fur glittered like a thousand tiny diamonds. Their sapphire-like eyes twinkled with purpose as they galloped gracefully with their tails and manes streaming behind them, the colors running together in a beautiful mix of blues and whites.

The carriage came to a halt in front of the Ice Castle's grand entrance. As I flung the door open, icy air slapped me in the face. My feet crunched on the winter-hardened earth as I leaped down. The castle's façade blazed with a crystalline blue that pricked my eyes after spending the last few days under the black skies of the Storm Castle.

"Helena!" Fannar called, his tone half exasperated, half amused. "You're supposed to wait for the footman!"

"Why wait when I can just jump down myself?" I grinned and waved a hand dismissively at the approaching footmen as my boots crunched on the snow-dusted cobblestones.

Fannar shook his head as he stepped down, the hint of a smile playing on his lips. "At least, let me get out first so *I* can help you down. Otherwise, people might think I'm an impolite asshole."

"Fine." I rolled my eyes with a laugh, linking my arm through his. "I promise to curb my impulsive nature so you can play the proper prince."

Adis welcomed me once we were inside. The king and queen had assigned her as my handmaid during my stay at the castle. She would be pleased to hear how happy Gwyneira was in the Storm Kingdom since she had previously served as Gwyneira's handmaid.

She brought me a large royal-blue velvet coat adorned with an intricate gold pattern along the edges and lined with soft white fur. She slipped it over my shoulders and clasped it around my neck. Ice Enchanted didn't need coats, but of course, I did.

I thanked her quietly before making my way back to Fannar's side. We made our way through the castle's vast halls, each room more breathtaking than the last. Towering ice sculptures, glittering like diamonds, lined the path to the throne room. Beautiful but cold . . . so fucking cold.

Fannar's smile faded as we ascended the stairs toward the throne room. He always tensed up when he was about to see his parents, their frosty formality leaching the warmth from him.

With a tug from the guards, the massive doors groaned open, and we stepped inside the cavernous throne room. Jagged icicles hung from the arched ceiling, refracting the sunlight into a thousand shimmering rainbows on the floor. The Ice King and Queen sat rigidly atop their glassy thrones, regal and aloof, epitomizing their kingdom's frozen majesty.

The queen's gown appeared to be pure frost, shimmering with her every movement. A crown of imposing spiked icicles adorned her long snow-white hair, which flowed like a frozen waterfall down her back. Her arctic blue eyes, set against her pale skin, burned into my soul like the icy grip of winter.

Beside her, the Ice King drew equal attention. Deep blue eyes that pointedly assessed everything accentuated his stern visage. He wore a crisply tailored navy-blue full dress military uniform with gleaming gold buttons. Numerous medals adorned his chest, showcasing his achievements and stature. His short silver hair, crowned by an intricately designed lattice of sparkling ice, enhanced his dignified appearance, capturing any daring light.

"Welcome back, Prince Fannar, Lady Helena," the Ice King greeted us with a curt nod, his voice devoid of warmth.

"Thank you, Your Majesties." Fannar bowed, and I curtsied alongside him.

"Father, Mother," Fannar began, his voice matching their detachment. "We are back from the Storm Kingdom and have important news to share."

"Proceed," the Ice Queen arched an eyebrow, her eyes never leaving ours and her face unreadable as always.

According to Fannar, his parents believed that showing emotions was a sign of weakness, so this aloof, reserved demeanor was expected of everyone here. I knew it was part of their culture, but it didn't mean I had to like it. Fortunately, they did not expect it from me.

I bit my tongue, longing to shatter their icy composure with some smart remark. But I knew my irreverence would only cause Fannar distress later.

"First, Gwyneira is very happy in the Storm Kingdom." Fannar's voice betrayed a subtle hint of fondness when saying his sister's name. "Brontes is treating her very well, and they are deeply in love."

The Ice Queen rolled her eyes.

"Is that all?" the Ice King asked dismissively, his cold stare not matching the warmth of the news. "You wasted your time visiting her when there are far more pressing matters?"

Fannar's hands clenched into fists. I could see the anger flickering beneath his carefully maintained composure. He cared deeply for Gwyneira, and their parents' indifference weighed on him. I placed a gentle hand on his arm, reminding him to stay calm and urging him to continue.

He took a deep breath, and his voice remained steady. "Brontes has become king of the Storm Kingdom after a successful coup on his parents."

"Oh." The Ice Queen glanced at the Ice King. "That is good news."

"Yes," the Ice King agreed. "As Storm King, his union with our daughter will now surely strengthen our alliance."

Fannar nodded. "Father, Mother, there's more. We've discovered a threat that must be addressed immediately."

The Ice King raised an eyebrow, remaining silent as he waited for more information.

Fannar glanced at me with determination behind his cool façade before he continued, "During our stay at the Storm Castle, we were attacked by a rogue Cosmic Enchanted named Obsidia. She intends to kill both Gwyneira and myself so she can have the Storm King to herself. We've come here seeking your help against this threat."

His parents listened impassively, no reaction betraying their thoughts as Fannar described the events of that morning at the Storm Castle. He made it clear that her intent was to kill him and Gwyneira, as well as conquer the Enchanted Realm.

When he finished, the Ice King and Ice Queen exchanged glances.

"The existence of more than one Cosmic Enchanted in the same realm is impossible," the Ice Queen said, narrowing her eyes, skepticism etched on her emotionless faces.

"Obsidia's powers are unlike anything we've ever seen," Fannar explained.

"There hasn't been a sorcerer of dark magic in decades," the Ice King added doubtfully. "Are you certain of these claims?"

I stepped forward, unable to hold my tongue any longer. "We know what we saw. She can create portals just like Headmaster Moira!"

"She was so powerful that she was able to fight Brontes, Helena, and me at the same time." Fannar's jaw tightened. "We barely escaped with our lives. She's a threat to both the Storm Kingdom and Ice Kingdom."

"She's dangerous and will stop at nothing to get what she wants," I pressed with urgency in my voice. "It's only a matter of time before she tries again."

The Ice King pondered our request in tense silence for a long minute before he spoke again. "We—"

A thunderous crash echoed through the hall, interrupting the Ice King. A swirling portal yawned open before us, and Obsidia stepped out, eyes aglow with dark purpose.

"Did you miss me, darlings?" she purred.

A blast of icy wind slammed into Obsidia, driving her back through the portal.

"Get back!" Fannar stood with one hand outstretched, frost swirling around his fingers while an ice dagger formed in his other fist.

"Guards!" the Ice King bellowed, and the room erupted into chaos as guards scrambled into the throne room.

A jagged bolt of shadow streaked over our heads, blasting apart the walls.

"Protect the King and Queen!" The commander shouted as debris rained down on us. The guards formed a barrier, brandishing their ice weapons, ready to defend the royal couple.

Obsidia strode from the portal, magic crackling around her. With a flick of her wrist, she seized two guards in coils of dark energy and hurled them aside. They hit the far wall and crumpled to the floor.

Fannar conjured a blizzard to obscure Obsidia's vision while the other Ice Enchanted tried to freeze her body to slow her movements, but she continued to advance toward us.

"Your efforts are futile," she taunted. "You cannot hope to defeat me!"

I swept my arm in an arc, sending a wall of fire roaring toward her. She dissolved it with a contemptuous wave, advancing slowly.

"Is that the best you can do, little spark? Your Ice Prince is as good as dead!" She lashed out, her dark energy sending me crashing through an ice pillar.

My veins pulsed as if a million volts of electricity were being released inside my blood, consuming me from within like an unnatural inferno. Pain exploded through my body as I tried to catch my breath on the cold floor.

"Helena!" Fannar's anguished cry pierced through the hall, and a wave of energy surged from him, shaking the castle walls.

My neck muscles tightened as I forced my chin up to look at him. His crystalline eyes blazed with rage as he stared down at me with intense worry etched into every angle of his face. I opened my mouth to let him know that I was okay, but it was too late.

It started as tiny sparks sizzling around his clenched fists before they quickly morphed into a raging inferno, erupting from his palms toward Obsidia.

"Ah, there's the Ice Prince's fiery temper," she mocked and easily deflected Fannar's flames as they spread across the throne room. "Don't worry, I'll reunite you with your Fire Princess in death soon enough!"

The thick walls of solid ice around us groaned as they began to melt under the disastrous combination of fire and black magic.

"Damn it!" Fannar muttered under his breath, trying to regain control, but he couldn't contain his own power as it spiraled outward in an inferno that threatened to consume the entire castle.

Cracks spider-webbed through the walls and ceiling. One of the walls collapsed around us from the intensity of the heat. Given how unstable the Ice Castle already was, my fire powers would only make the situation worse. Despite my injuries, I mustered all my strength to extinguish the flames Fannar had created, and my body weakened even more.

Obsidia raised her arms, summoning a swirling vortex overhead, aiming toward Fannar.

"She's after Fannar!" I pleaded to the guards desperately, but I knew their duty was to protect the king and queen above all else.

Chunks of ice broke free of the ceiling, crashing down around us. The remaining guards closed ranks around the king and queen, shielding them with their bodies.

I clutched my injured side, willing the pain away. We had to stop Obsidia before she could hurt anyone else.

Fannar gave me a grim look, and I nodded in silent agreement. We had one chance. Calling on every last bit of strength, we unleashed our powers as one. With a roar, I opened my arms wide, and a wave of flames exploded from the depths of my being, searing everything in its path. Fannar summoned countless shards of ice from the air, freezing our enemies in their tracks. Together, our attacks created a swirling vortex of searing heat and icy chill that surged toward Obsidia.

Her eyes widened in surprise before she crossed her arms over her face, weathering the assault. She slid back inch by inch, heels carving furrows in the floor.

"Is that all you have?" she panted.

The castle trembled under the elemental onslaught.

With a gasp, my flames sputtered out. Beside me, Fannar sagged to one knee, ice melting from his hands. We were spent. And Obsidia still stood through sheer force of will, darkness writhing around her.

She flung out a hand, sending us both flying into the remaining guards. We tumbled to the floor in a heap.

"Pathetic," Obsidia sneered. "I expected more of a challenge from the legendary storm of fire and ice."

She strode toward us, murder in her eyes. I struggled to rise, to defend Fannar, but my limbs refused to obey. This was it. We had failed.

"Your fight is with us, witch!" The Ice King bellowed.

A massive chunk of the ceiling crashed down. Obsidia glanced up in surprise as more debris rained around her until she was buried in a large pile of ice.

The Ice King and Queen strode into view, ice swirling around them.

“That won’t hold her for long!” The Ice Queen glared at us and pointed to the exit. “You must go!”

“Yes.” The Ice King nodded defiantly. “We’ll hold her off while you and Helena escape.”

“No!” Fannar shouted. “We won’t leave you.”

“Fannar, you are the heir to this kingdom,” his father reminded him sternly. “You must survive to lead our people.”

“But both of you must come with us!” Desperation was clear in Fannar’s voice.

A deep purple hue emanated from the pile of ice that held Obsidia in place. It quaked from within. The king and queen blasted it with icy gusts of wind to keep the pile solidified for as long as they could.

“My son,” the Ice Queen said, “we must stay to protect our people as long as we can. You must go now!”

“You four guards! Escort the Prince and his lady out of the castle immediately!” The king glowered at us, but his firm gaze was tinged with softness. “Take them by force, if necessary, and do not return until they are safe.”

“Yes, Your Majesty!” The guards pointed their icy spears at us.

“Father!” Fannar protested one last time.

The Ice Queen touched my arm. “Take care of him, Helena. The future of the Ice Kingdom depends on him.”

I nodded, fighting to hold back the tears in my eyes, and grabbed Fannar's hand as the guards led us away from the chaos.

As we made our way through the crumbling halls, I stumbled, my injured side protesting the sudden movement. Fannar caught me, pulling me up and urging me to keep going. His arm around my waist and the sheer determination emanating from him were the only things keeping me from collapsing completely.

The sounds of battle and destruction raged above us, and my heart ached with guilt at leaving the king and queen behind. But I knew they were right. The Ice Kingdom would fall if Obsidia defeated all three of them. Fannar was the future of this kingdom.

"We have to keep moving." Fannar's hand tightened around mine, his knuckles white with the pressure. "We have to get to the carriage."

I nodded, my determination renewed. I had to make sure Fannar survived for the sake of the Ice Kingdom.

Once outside, the guards shoved us into a waiting carriage, the same one we had arrived in.

"Quickly!" one of the guards urged as the others took up positions around our carriage, ready to fend off any attackers.

"Hyah!" The driver shouted. The unicorns neighed nervously before finally pulling away as fast as their hooves could carry us.

A deafening crack ripped through the sky. Whirling around, I peered out the back window of the carriage at an ominous aura erupting from the top of the Ice Castle. Great shards of ice splintered off in exploding plumes, raining down onto the hard-packed snow below like icy shrapnel.

My hands clutched Fannar's sleeve as a towering spire that had stood for centuries wobbled with a horrendous snap. It plunged earthward, dragging frozen battlements down with it, and obliterated an entire colonnade in an avalanche of crystalline debris.

The shattering and crashing of ice cut through the tranquility of what had been a serene afternoon. With every collapse of another magnificent turret, splintered balcony, and fallen wall, a cold fist closed around my heart as I thought about the number of lives that may have been lost.

Horrified yet unable to tear my eyes away, the majestic Ice Castle crumbled down in slow motion like a nightmare, its brilliant blue walls becoming obscured by a dark purple fog before tumbling to the ground with the rest of Fannar's childhood home.

The Ice Castle was gone.

My hands trembled as I clung to Fannar tightly. Tears streamed down my face.

"Your parents . . ." I whispered.

The unicorns galloped down the mountain path, putting distance between us and the destroyed castle. I clenched my fists, nails digging into my palms. A tiny flame sparked to life in my hand, flickering with my raw emotion. Snuffing it out, I forced myself to regain control.

"Take us to Haven Academy," Fannar said to the driver, ignoring me. His face was a stony mask etched with determination. I knew he was trying to be strong, to do his duty and get us to safety. But I could see the anguish in his eyes. His parents had never been warm, but they were still his family. And now they were gone.

CHAPTER FIVE
GWYNEIRA

Since I was a little girl, I'd dreamt of the day Fannar and I would arrive at Haven Academy together. In my daydreams, we would walk through its grand doors wearing crisp new uniforms, and he would proudly introduce me to his friends and the faculty members.

But now, as the Storm Kingdom's royal carriage approached the academy, I couldn't believe Brontes and I would be visiting for the first time under such dire circumstances.

"Never thought we'd come here like this, huh?" Brontes said, as if he sensed my thoughts. His strong hand squeezed mine, offering comfort in these dark times.

"No, not like this," I replied, my voice barely audible.

The shiny onyx carriage towed by Elias's four best black stallions fit in perfectly with the impressive gothic architecture that loomed before us.

The exterior reminded me of a magnificent cathedral with large spires and arched stained-glass windows that sparkled in the daylight. The stone walls rose high into the sky, adorned with intricate carvings of mythical creatures, including gargoyles perched on the crowns and grinning down at us. Birds cawed in the sky as we approached the door, and the sun cast warm shadows from the trees onto our path.

In the front of the academy's imposing entrance stood a striking woman garbed in a frilly, opulent dress of deep royal purple. The voluminous skirt billowed around her knees, reminiscent of a bygone era. Delicate black lace adorned the hem and cuffs in intricate patterns. Velvet ribbons and bows added a touch of playful elegance, completing her eccentric but regal ensemble.

Her lacy black parasol, unfurled like a dark bloom, shielded her from the sun's rays. Thick black eyelashes and deep plum lipstick contrasted sharply against her porcelain white skin. She wore her jet-black hair coiled meticulously into a sleek and glossy bun.

"Welcome to Haven Academy at Henristead, King Brontes and Princess Gwyneira." Her voice, velvety yet commanding, broke the silence. "I am Headmaster Moira."

"Headmaster Moira," Brontes stepped forward and bowed slightly. "Thank you for receiving us so promptly."

"Of course. I wish it were under better circumstances," she replied and turned to me. "My condolences for the attack in the Ice Kingdom."

I shuddered at her words, imagining the fall of the Ice Castle again. As soon as Fannar and Helena had arrived at Haven Academy, Headmaster Moira had called Brontes in the Storm Kingdom to relay what had happened. We came as quickly as we could.

My heart ached for my parents, for our people, and for Fannar, who had been forced to bear the weight of it all. I allowed myself to remain detached from the possible loss of our parents. I needed to be strong for Fannar. Helena was hurt, and . . . he might be king now.

"Please follow me," Headmaster Moira said, gesturing for us to follow her into the academy.

The large oak doors creaked open, revealing the academy's interior, lit by glowing orbs that cast eerie shadows on the floor.

"Helena is still recovering in the Healing Center with Fannar." Headmaster Moira led us through the labyrinthine corridors of Haven Academy.

"Did they tell you about Obsidia?" Brontes asked.

"The other Cosmic Enchanted, yes." She nodded once, concern lacing her reply. "But not much. We had to rush Helena to the Healing Center due to her injuries."

"Oh no! Are they that bad?" I asked with alarm.

"She will recover fully. Our healers are the best in the realm."

We arrived at the Healing Center, a large, cavernous chamber decorated with a kaleidoscope of colorful stained glass windows. The inside looked even more like a cathedral than the outside of the academy, but filled with beds and medical equipment instead of pews.

I spotted Fannar sitting in a chair near the front of the room in a small waiting area. His face was etched with fatigue, as if he hadn't slept in days, and his eyes held a haunted expression I had never seen before. As we approached, he stood up, trying to regain his usual stoic composure. My chest tightened at the sight of his pain.

"Brother!" I rushed over and threw my arms around him, holding him tight.

His strong arms embraced me, offering comfort in a world that had crumbled around us. "Sister, I'm so glad you're safe."

"Nurse?" Headmaster Moira turned to a nearby nurse, who had mantis-like arms extending from her torso.

The insectoid limbs were both fascinating and unnerving, but there was a gentle quality in the nurse's eyes that softened her appearance.

"How is Helena doing?" Headmaster Moira asked.

"She's with the healer now." The nurse looked at her watch. "Her treatment should be finished soon. She's recovering well."

"Good." The headmaster nodded and turned back to us. "Once Helena is released, come to my office so we can discuss arrangements for the four of you." With that, she strode out of the room, her heels clicking against the stone floor.

Fannar turned to Brontes. "Thank you for coming so quickly."

"Of course," Brontes replied. "I couldn't leave you and Gwyneira alone in this time of need."

"What about your kingdom?"

"Fortunately, Gwyneira and I were able to select a handful of trusted advisors before we left. The Storm Kingdom is in safe hands for now." Brontes's eyebrows knitted together in sympathy, and he frowned. "Fannar, I'm so sorry about your home and your parents."

Fannar nodded appreciatively. "Can't believe they're gone," he whispered as his eyes clouded with sorrow. He stared down at his hands. "I summoned fire accidentally . . . I couldn't control it. I might as well have helped Obsidia burn down the Ice Castle. I should've—"

"No, brother," I said firmly and grasped his hands. "Don't go there."

Fannar and I sat down next to each other, our shared grief weighing heavily on us. His jaw was clenched, his eyes hard. I knew he was holding back a storm of emotion—grief, anger, guilt. He blamed himself for not being able to protect our parents, our home, our kingdom. I wished he would let me comfort him, let me share his pain instead of bearing it alone. But he remained locked behind the walls he had built long ago, walls I could not seem to b reach.

I reached for his hand. He glanced down in surprise, then gave my hand a small squeeze. It wasn't much, but for now it would have to be enough just to find solace in one another's presence. I fought to hold back the tears that threatened to spill over, while Fannar's stoicism remained unbroken.

"We will make sure their sacrifice was not in vain," Fannar promised. "We'll make them proud."

"Yes, we will," I agreed, drawing strength from his conviction. "All of us. Together."

He pulled me into another tight embrace, our shared pain forming an unbreakable bond between us. Though no tears fell, our hearts ached in unison as we grieved.

The door to one of inner rooms swung open, and Helena emerged, her abdomen wrapped tightly in bandages underneath her sports bra. Fannar practically leaped out of his chair, sprinting over to her before I could blink.

"Helena, are you okay?" His hands gently held her arms, eagerness and concern written all over his face. He inspected her from head to toe as if he were looking for permanent damage.

"I'm alright, Fannar," Helena reassured him softly with a warm smile.

He let out a relieved sigh and cupped her cheeks in his hands. Their eyes locked together with softness and warmth that spoke volumes about the depth of their connection.

"Gwyn! Brontes!" Helena finally exclaimed after spotting me and Brontes.

"Helena, how are you feeling?" I stepped forward to greet her.

"Better now that you're here!" she replied cheerfully.

"We're happy to see you too," Brontes added.

She wrapped me in a tight hug and then immediately pulled away with a pained gasp, clutching her wounded side. "Ow! That hurt."

"Take it easy, okay?" Fannar said, concern evident in his voice as he touched her arm again.

Brontes chuckled.

"Fannar, your pants," Helena observed.

Fannar's leg had been injured during the attack, so one of his pant legs had a slit cut up to his thigh in order for the wound to be treated.

"It's fine," Fannar said. "They already healed."

"If you yank on them, do you think they'll come off like stripper pants?" Helena teased and then proceeded to laugh loudly at her own joke.

"Not funny." Fannar's brows scrunched in disapproval, but a small smile tugged on the corners of his mouth.

I giggled. Helena's fiery spirit obviously remained intact. I admired her more than ever in that moment—her strength, her courage, her refusal to be broken by any circumstance.

"Headmaster Moira wants to see all of us once you're released," Brontes informed Helena.

"Good, I'm so done with this place." Helena replied, her sassy attitude undiminished by her injuries. "I owe a Cosmic Enchanted an ass kicking."

Sometimes Helena's cursing still startled me, since swearing was forbidden in the Ice Castle. I found it hilarious that my reserved, uptight brother fell in love with such an outspoken woman who used profanity whenever she pleased and lived as if rules were meant to be broken.

"Still as stubborn as ever," Fannar chided. "You still need to be discharged by the nurse before we can leave."

Helena glanced over at the nurse, her eyes lingering on the nurse's mantis arms as she flipped through the pages on a clipboard. Helena leaned over to whisper in my ear. "I know it's mean, but her arms freak me out!"

I giggled again.

The nurse approached us, her eyes on Helena. "You can leave now, but you need to take it easy for the next day," she warned. "Your wound is healed, but since it was a dark magic burn, you'll still be sore."

"Okay, nurse," Helena nodded in understanding. "Thank you."

Fannar's gaze never left her, his concern for her evident in the crease between his brows and the way he hovered close. Relief washed over him when the nurse confirmed that Helena would be all right, and he reached out to place a gentle hand on her shoulder.

"Promise me you'll listen to the nurse," Fannar urged. His voice held a tender insistence, his eyes locked onto hers.

"Cross my heart," Helena winked, drawing an *X* over her chest with her finger.

"You winked!" Fannar protested.

"Fine! I promise!" Helena relented.

We all laughed and made our way out of the Healing Center. By then, the sun was setting, and the sky had taken on a rosy hue as we walked toward the main building. The majestic stone towers and ornate spires reaching toward the heavens paired with lush green gardens, making the academy an awe-inspiring sight.

Along the way, Fannar and Helena pointed out various points of interest to Brontes and me, including the famous academy library that I'd heard so much about. Despite the situation, I could barely contain my excitement about finally visiting it for the first time.

CHAPTER SIX
HELENA

Gwyneira and Fannar sat stiffly in the high-backed chairs, perched on the edge of their seats, hands clasped in their laps, and eyes fixed to Headmaster Moira's imposing mahogany desk. Brontes and I paced restlessly around her office, picking up trinkets and setting them back down. None of those objects would have the answers we sought.

Together, we recounted Obsidia's ruthless attacks on the Storm and Ice Castles. Reliving those tragic moments, the memories so vivid and fresh, pain ripped through me like a dagger. The Ice Castle had been my home for the past week, and despite all their flaws, the Ice King and Queen had graciously welcomed me. My heart filled with despair for Gwyneira and Fannar at their loss, but it quickly burned with hatred toward Obsidia, the destroyer of this family I had grown to love.

"Headmaster Moira, do you know anything about this Obsidia?" I asked eagerly. "Or even the existence of another Cosmic Enchanted in the Enchanted Realm?"

The headmaster's eyes narrowed, her lips pursed into a thin line. "I've never heard of her," she admitted, her voice heavy with concern. "While you were in the Healing Center, I did some digging and found no record of her. I *should be* the only Cosmic Enchanted, but, if Obsidia truly traveled from another dimension, it seems she has bent the rules."

"How is that even possible?" Brontes asked, trying to wrap his head around the concept. "That someone can just bend the rules like that?"

"How indeed?" Headmaster Moira continued, her voice steady yet filled with unease. "Cosmic Enchanted can teleport from one place to another, but we shouldn't be able to travel through time or between alternate realities."

"Could it be dark magic?" Fannar muttered, his eyes narrowing.

"Yes, that's right," I added. "The nurse said our wounds looked like they were burns from dark magic."

"Obsidia must have obtained that power through the dark magic she wields." Headmaster Moira leaned forward, her gaze shifting between us. "Did any of you notice a magical object she might have used?"

"Like what?" I asked.

"A staff? A wand? An orb?" The headmaster offered. "Anything that emitted light or energy?"

"Um . . ." Gwyneira hesitated before speaking up, her voice soft but clear. "I noticed Obsidia wore a brooch on her dress. It was black in the shape of a rose. It had this purplish glow from time to time when she used her powers."

"Good catch, Gwyn." I touched her shoulder with encouragement.

"Interesting," Headmaster Moira mused, her eyes narrowing. "It's likely a dark magic talisman."

"Do you know anything about it?" Brontes asked. "Perhaps it has a weakness that will help us defeat her."

The headmaster nodded. "I will look into it and see if I can find out more." Her brow furrowed as she pondered further. "But if this brooch only exists in Obsidia's world, we might be in for quite the challenge."

"The fall of the Ice Castle is just the beginning," Fannar chimed in, his expression stone-cold. "She won't stop until she conquers our entire realm."

If we couldn't figure out how to stop her, who knew what chaos she'd bring next? I glanced at everyone else's face. The weight of the headmaster's words settled heavily upon us, and they all looked as worried as I felt. Our worlds had been turned upside down, and no one was safe anymore.

"We will find a way to stop her," Gwyneira said softly but with firm resolve.

I reached out and squeezed Fannar's hand, drawing strength from his cool touch.

"Yes, whatever it takes," I added.

Headmaster Moira scanned each of our faces. "What do you want to do in the meantime?"

"Obsidia is after us." Brontes clenched his jaw and furrowed his brows as he glanced at Gwyneira and Fannar. "I don't want to endanger my people by returning to the Storm Kingdom and she attacks us again."

"Nor can we allow her to destroy the Storm Castle too." Gwyneira's shimmered with a fierce resolve.

"Obviously, there is no Ice Castle to go home to either." Fannar cupped his face in his hands.

"Headmaster, can we stay here for now?" I suggested. "That way, we can train our powers and be ready for the next fight."

"And use the library to see what else we can find," Gwyneira said.

"You mean, bring this rogue Cosmic Enchanted to the academy's doorstep?" Headmaster Moira retorted with astonishment.

"You're the only Cosmic Enchanted," I rebutted. "You said so yourself. We don't stand a chance without your help."

"This is probably the best place to face Obsidia and prevent casualties," Brontes remarked. "Class is not session for another week, and nearly all the students have returned home."

"That's true," Fannar agreed. "It's like a ghost town right now."

Headmaster Moira's eyes softened as she considered our request, and after a moment of contemplation, she nodded solemnly. "I understand your concerns, and while I would prefer not to bring the fight to Haven Academy, it seems we have no other choice. You may stay."

A collective sigh of relief escaped us, and some of the tension gradually dissipated from the room. Gratitude swelled in my chest, and I knew that my friends felt the same way.

An overwhelming sense of relief washed over me, and I noticed a similar look of gratitude on Gwyneira's face as she clutched Brontes's hand tightly. As much as we were venturing into the unknown, it was comforting to know that we had each other—and now, the support of someone as powerful as Headmaster Moira.

"As long as you're here, I'll do everything in my power to keep you all safe. We'll face Obsidia together."

"Thank you, Headmaster," Gwyneira whispered, her earlier apprehension replaced by a glimmer of hope.

"We are grateful for your support and hospitality." Brontes inclined his head respectfully. "The Storm Kingdom is in your debt."

"We'll do all we can to lessen the danger posed to the academy," Fannar promised.

"Yes, of course," Headmaster Moira waved a hand as if already dismissing the danger. "As for accommodations, I have some empty dorm rooms where you can stay. Gwyneira, there's a vacant space in the girls' dormitory, and Brontes, you can take one in the boys' dormitory."

"Actually," I interjected, seizing the opportunity, "Gwyneira can stay in my room. My roommate went home for winter break, so there's plenty of space."

"Very well," Headmaster Moira agreed, her gaze softening for a brief moment before returning to its usual sternness. "But do ensure that you both get the rest you need. We'll need all our strength and wits about us in the coming days."

"Yes, ma'am!" we chorused.

As we left the headmaster's office, the door creaking shut behind us, I leaned in conspiratorially.

"Listen, you two can both stay in my room," I whispered, my eyes dancing with mischief.

"Helena!" Gwyneira gasped, her cheeks turning a lovely shade of pink.

"Relax, it'll be fine!" I winked. "I've been sleeping in Fannar's room almost every night for a long time now, but we won't tell Moira that." I grinned at Fannar, who looked both amused and exasperated.

Brontes chuckled. "I was going to say that it's been a long time since either Gwyneira and I slept apart from each other."

Gwyneira hesitated for a moment before finally relenting, offering me a small, grateful smile. "Yes, thank you."

"No problem! I trust you two to behave yourselves." I winked at the both of them.

"Gross!" Fannar exclaimed. "She's my little sister!"

"What?! I didn't say anything!"

We all laughed as we made our way to the dorms.

It was so weird to be walking through the Academy without all the students. I'd become so used to being shoulder to shoulder with plum blazers that the corridors looked a hundred feet wide with only the four of us in them. The usual hustle and bustle of Haven Academy had been replaced by a desolate stillness.

According to the headmaster, there were supposedly a handful of other strays like us, but we rarely crossed paths with them. The dining hall was also eerily quiet, only the distant clatter of pots and pans echoing through the vast space as Frankie the chef gremlin worked his literal culinary magic.

We sat together at a long table, its polished wooden surface gleaming beneath the harsh glow of the florescent lights overhead. The worn dining chairs creaked under our weight, each one telling its own story of past conversations.

"Kinda strange to see this place so empty, huh?" I mused, twirling a forkful of spaghetti around my fork.

The aroma of garlic and tomatoes filled the air, while the savory steam from the roasted vegetables and grilled chicken wafted between us. Despite the lack of company, Frankie hadn't skimped on the quality or quantity of our meal.

"At least we're not starving, right? We still have Frankie," I said. Fannar gave me an approving smirk, a dollop of mashed potatoes precariously teetering on his spoon. He glanced across the table at Brontes and Gwyneira.

"So how do you like the food?"

"It's delicious!" Gwyneira's eyes lit up with excitement as she looked over her plate. "Just being here is wonderful! I never thought I'd get to eat at the academy dining hall."

She proudly dug into her multicolored roasted vegetables with gusto. The steam rising up from her grilled chicken added a savory aroma of juicy meat and rosemary to the air.

"The food is amazing here." Brontes gave a nod of approval before stuffing his mouth full of pasta.

"Glad you like it so far." I took a sip of my soda.

"Unfortunately, you're not getting the full academy experience without the rest of our classmates, but we've got to make the most of it, right?" Fannar smiled softly.

My gaze fell on the array of condiments lining the center of the table, their vibrant colors inviting mischief.

A wicked grin spread across my face as an idea took root. "Why don't we liven things up a bit? Who's up for a fun challenge?"

Brontes's eyes grew wide as he leaned in with curiosity. "What kind of challenge?"

"A hot sauce challenge! I'm going to mix every sauce here." I gathered up the various bottles and began to pour a little bit of each one into a small glass, creating an alarming molten-red concoction that bubbled and fizzed. "And I dare you to take a sip!"

"Are you insane?" Fannar scoffed, raising an eyebrow at the spiciest hot sauce in particular.

"What's the matter, Ice Prince?" I taunted. "Afraid of a little heat?"

"Yeah, my powers won't be enough to cool me down after that."

"Aw, come on! Live a little," I teased, nudging him playfully with my elbow.

Gwyneira giggled at our banter until Brontes chimed in.

"I accept your challenge!" Brontes exclaimed.

Gwyneira's eyes widened. "Brontes, maybe we should think this through . . ." She touched his arm gently, trying to be the voice of reason. "I don't want you to get sick when we just got here."

"The Storm King fears no sauce!" he declared with bravado.

"This might not be the best idea," she warned.

But it was too late. He was already lifting the glass to his lips. He gulped down the mixture in one swig.

Instantly, his face transformed into a cherry-red canvas of comical agony as tears pooled in his eyes and beads of sweat dotted his temples. His fiery panting could have given any dragon a run for its money.

My hands flew over my mouth in shock—or attempting to stifle laughter—I'm not sure which.

"Wow," Fannar remarked as he watched Brontes struggle to catch his breath. He patted Brontes on the back.

"Are you okay?" Gwyneira handed him a glass of water, genuine concern etched on her face.

"Never . . . better . . ." Brontes wheezed, grinning through the obvious pain before gulping down the entire glass.

Fannar winced at the spectacle. "Was it worth it to impress Gwyneira?" he asked wryly.

Brontes feigned nonchalance, shooting her a blinding grin through watering eyes. "Always."

"Silly Brontes." Gwyneira blushed deeply but took his hand.

Laughter erupted in our cozy corner, the sound bouncing off the walls. Our shared amusement lightened our hearts, allowing us to briefly forget the chaotic day. For that fleeting moment, things felt normal.

Just as our laughter started to die down, Headmaster Moira approached our table. A nameless knot of dread formed in my gut, tightening as she neared. Everyone knew that if Headmaster Moira wanted to speak to you, she called you to her office. She never came to you. If the headmaster sought us out, it had to be serious.

"Good evening, everyone," she greeted with a low murmur that cloaked the room in a new level of eerie silence. "There's been a development in the Ice Kingdom."

My heart leaped into my throat, but my focus turned to Gwyneira and Fannar. Their usual controlled exterior rippled for a moment at the headmaster's words. We exchanged worried glances as we braced ourselves for whatever she was about to share.

Headmaster Moira's eyes softened, as if reading my thoughts. "The Ice King and Queen survived. I finally managed to speak with them through a projection portal."

"How is that possible?" Fannar's usually calm demeanor fractured as disbelief glazed his voice. "We saw the Ice Castle collapse."

"Obsidia teleported out of the castle as soon as she realized the two of you were gone." Headmaster Moira's tone held notes of admiration as she answered, "Your parents and their guards combined their powers to form a thick ice barrier that shielded them and a handful of others from the castle's collapse."

As the relief washed over us, we remained silent, taking in the aftermath of the shock.

"Of course, there are injuries among the castle staff," Headmaster Moira continued, surrendering more details. "But everyone is expected to make a full recovery. Some of the townspeople have taken upon themselves to begin reconstruction of the castle."

I breathed a sigh of relief as the weight of grief lifted from my chest.

Gwyneira spoke first, joy sparkling in her cerulean eyes. "Headmaster, thank you for this news."

"Yes, thank you," Fannar quickly added.

"Your people are strong and resilient," Headmaster Moira nodded, her words delivering a warm conviction that seeped into us. "Now, get some rest. You've all had a long day, and we still have much to do. Keep your spirits high, my dears, for hope is never lost."

As she left, we shared teary smiles. Gwyneira collapsed into Brontes's arms, burying her glistening face into his chest. Fannar's hand found mine under the table, and we squeezed each other's hands for reassurance. Fannar let out a long breath, shoulders relaxing. My own eyes burned, the ever-present knot in my chest finally loosening.

We collected our belongings, leaving behind the cavernous cafeteria with renewed hope. The day ended on a far happier note than I could've imagined. But as we made our way back to the dorms, I glanced at Fannar.

His eyes were fixed ahead as he walked stiffly, his arms crossed tightly over his chest as if trying to stifle whatever emotions he was feeling. But I knew better than to press him in front of the others.

We said our goodnights to Gwyneira and Brontes, parting ways with them as they headed to my dorm room. Fannar and I continued to his room. He opened the door, ushering me in before him.

"What is it?" I asked as soon as he closed the door behind him. "You just found out your parents are still alive. What gives?"

Fannar sighed heavily and looked away from me. He was clearly struggling with something, but I couldn't tell what it was.

A sudden chill in the room hit me immediately. I rubbed my arms, glancing around to see if it was the A/C.

"Fannar," I said softly.

He didn't respond, his pale blue eyes darting around the room as if searching for an escape. He picked up a book from his desk, flipping through the pages without really reading them before adjusting an already straight picture frame on the wall.

The temperature dropped further, and my breath turned to fog. He was unintentionally cooling the room again. Time for a different tactic.

"Jeez, babe, save some cold for the Ice Kingdom," I quipped, trying to lighten the mood. "I'm gonna need a parka in here soon."

Still nothing. Not even a hint of a smile.

Instead, his jaw clenched, and he shuffled a random stack of papers on his desk.

I moved closer, reaching out to place my hand on his arm. "Babe, look at me."

He glanced at me quickly, betraying the unshed tears in his eyes, before shifting his gaze away again.

"Talk to me, Fannar," I urged, wrapping my fingers around his wrist, tugging gently to draw his attention back to me. I guided him to sit on the bed next to me. "Please, you don't have to hide anything from me."

His eyes met mine again, and the façade Fannar held onto so desperately began to crack. His voice trembled as he finally spoke, "They almost died because of me . . . trying to protect us." He let out a choked sob, the dam finally breaking. "I should have protected *them*."

A tear trickled down his cheek, and my heart caught in my throat at the sight of it. I wrapped my arms around him, drawing his head against my chest, and he clung onto me tightly.

"Shhh," I soothed. "It's not your fault. We did everything we could."

"We should have never left." He shook his head. "This whole day, I thought they were gone. I should have known. We should have searched for them—"

"Stop it," I chided, stroking his soft white hair. "They wanted to protect you because you're the future of the Ice Kingdom. They know how important you are. They said so themselves, Fannar."

As I held him, his tears stopped, but he still clung to me like a lifeline as his breathing evened out. The cold air around us gradually dissipated as his head pressed against me. I breathed in his crisp scent of freshly fallen snow.

"I should have been stronger," he muttered into my chest.

I gently lifted his chin so his eyes, red-rimmed but finally clear, met mine. "Babe, you're one of the strongest people I know."

Fannar chuckled and smiled softly. "I was going to say that about you." He took a shuddering breath to compose himself before pressing his forehead to mine and closing his eyes. “I really love you, you know.”

“I know.” I smirked. “I love you too.”

We came together in a soft, lingering kiss—gentle yet filled with a thousand unspoken words. His hands came up to cradle my face as he deepened the kiss.

Our bodies melded together as if our souls were hungry for one another, the intensity between us slowly building. His hands dropped down my body, exploring every inch of me as our kiss became more passionate and urgent. Heat rushed through me like a wildfire, every nerve ending alive with longing and anticipation.

With a gentle growl of pleasure, his hands roamed even further up my body and cupped my breasts. His arousal pressed against me, sending a jolt down to my core. We wanted each other in a way that was almost primal. The desire surging between us was almost too powerful to resist.

I pulled his shirt off over his head, and I slid my hands over his hard chest, his heart beating wildly under my palm. His muscles rippled beneath my fingertips, begging to be touched. I took a deep breath, inhaling his wintery scent again, and traced my fingers along the ridges of his abdomen.

His lips moved hungrily across mine as our tongues caressed each other. I wanted him. All of him. I needed him satisfied and sated, his desire for me greater than his desperation to protect me.

As I gazed into his eyes and his smoldering gaze held mine like a magnet, Fannar's fingers dipped underneath my skirt and found the delicate lace of my panties, sliding beneath the fabric and teasing the slick heat that awaited him. My breath hitched as he expertly pulled them off.

He held my hands in his, helping me to climb onto his lap. I straddled him, my bare legs pressing into him as I ground against him. His erection hardened beneath me, and a hungry growl rumbled in his chest.

After I pulled my shirt off, he began kissing down my chest, taking his time to caress me with his hands and mouth. He cupped my breasts, tugging at my nipples softly, eagerly watching the way they pebbled at his touch. His cold tongue traced circles around my nipples before he sucked one into his mouth, causing me to shudder in pleasure. My back arched involuntarily, pressing my breast deeper into his mouth, my body suddenly feeling hot all ov er.

"Fannar," I gasped, the sensation of his tongue and teeth teasing my sensitive flesh overwhelming me. He switched his attention to my other breast, lavishing it with equal fervor, his fingers rolling and pinching the abandoned nipple. The dual assault had me writhing beneath him, my hips grinding against his in search of relief.

Reaching down, I stroked his hardness through his pants, feeling how ready he was for me. I undid the clasp of his pants and pushed them down slowly, reveling in the sight of his massive erection springing free.

Crouching down on the floor, I gazed up at him and took his sweetness into my mouth as far as I could.

He moaned and bucked his hips toward me. Relishing the sound of his approval, I bobbed my head up and down, sucking him in a slow, rhythmic motion as my tongue swirled around his shaft.

He grunted, his hands gripping my hair tightly. He pushed his hips toward me, urging me to pick up the pace.

And I did. I took him in deeper with each downward movement.

His member throbbed and pulsated in my mouth. I could feel his heartbeat against my lips and tongue. I wanted to make him feel good. I wanted him to want nothing but me.

And judging by his moans and the way his face looked, I was doing a pretty damn good job.

He groaned again. He was loving this. He was loving the way I was worshipping his manhood with my mouth.

Suddenly, he pulled my head back. "That's enough."

He lifted me onto the desk, his hands on my hips, and I could feel his desire for me.

"Tell me what you want, Helena," he whispered, his breath tickling my ear.

"I need you inside me," I begged, the anticipation threatening to consume me. I spread my legs, offering myself to him as I looked up with need in my eyes.

He positioned himself at my entrance and pushed inside with one swift, forceful thrust. I gasped at the fullness, every inch of him stretching me, taking my breath away.

"Helena," he groaned, his own desire mirrored in the tortured sound as his length drove into my core.

His hips moved with fevered purpose, slamming into me over and over. I met his strokes, matching his intensity, my nails digging into his shoulders.

"Fannar!" I cried out his name, echoing his grunts of pleasure.

"You're so beautiful," he groaned, his voice low and husky.

He moved his hips faster, pumping into me harder, causing me to see stars. Our bodies became one, our breathing ragged. He pulled back, watching the disappointment and confusion in my face, before plunging back inside without warning.

"Gods, Helena," he panted, his voice rough with lust. "You're so damn tight."

His hand found my sensitive nub, rubbing it in time with his thrusts, sending shockwaves of pleasure coursing through my body. I arched into his irresistible touch, my nails carving red marks into his skin.

The world around us seemed to fall away as we lost ourselves in each other, our love manifesting in the raw, primal dance of passion that bound us together. With every stroke, every gasp and moan, we shared not just our bodies, but our hearts and souls, forging an unbreakable connection that transcended time and space.

His hands gripped my rear tightly as he pounded into me, his manhood finding that sweet spot of mine with each powerful thrust.

"Oh, babe!" I cried out breathlessly.

My eyes rolled back in my head, my mouth open in a silent scream. My world became consumed by sensation—the feeling of being taken, owned, and loved.

As the climax approached, the tension between us snapped like a tightly wound coil, sending waves of euphoria crashing through my body. My inner walls clenched around him as he emptied himself into me, milking his shaft until he filled me completely.

He collapsed on top of me, panting heavily, and I clung to him, our bodies shuddering in ecstasy.

CHAPTER SEVEN
GWYNEIRA

The sun's rays shone brightly over the distant mountains as I stepped outside into the crisp morning air. The light breeze was tinged with the scent of dew-kissed grass and fresh flowers. I marveled at the way the Storm Guild kept Haven Academy's weather consistently pleasant, no matter the time of year. I believed we could do the same at the Storm Castle, but I'd grown to appreciate the dynamic weather of the Storm Kingdom.

Brontes, Fannar, and Helena made their way across the sprawling campus grounds toward the library as I followed behind them. The weight of our mission grew heavier, pressing down on my shoulders with each step. We had to find something, anything, to defeat Obsidia before she could unleash her darkness upon our realm.

I balled my hands into fists, anger swelling within me. I refused to let that witch hurt my friends and family. She wanted me, for whatever twisted prophecy she believed I was part of, as a way to get to Brontes. I wouldn't let her use me to harm those I loved, especially not *my* Brontes.

My heart flared as I stole a glance at Brontes chatting with Helena and Fannar.

As long as I live, Obsidia will never have him.

Since I was her main target, I knew the guys constantly worried about me. I felt like an unbearable burden on them all, even Helena. I vowed to train harder, become stronger, so they would all see that I could protect myself.

I pushed those thoughts away for now, instead taking in everything around me. The sun shined brightly on the bold stone walls of Haven Academy, bathing us in its rays of warmth. Anticipation bubbled up inside me. I'd dreamed of coming here for so long. And now, despite the looming threat, finally being here seemed so surreal.

When we entered the grand library, the sight that greeted us was nothing short of awe-inspiring. Fannar had told me countless stories about the library's vast collection, but nothing could have prepared me for actually seeing it myself. Crystal chandeliers hanging from the vaulted ceiling cast prismatic rainbows across the marble floors. The massive picture windows let in warm sunlight, bathing the room in gold.

I spun in a slow circle, taking it all in. Towering shelves stretched up into shadowed heights, the faint scent of leather and parchment enveloping me. A boundless universe of knowledge surrounded us, waiting to be explored.

"Wow," I whispered. "It's magical!"

Helena guffawed loudly and smiled at me. "I've never seen anyone so mesmerized by a bunch of books."

Brontes gazed down at me with a sweet smile and gently rubbed the small of my back, as if to say he understood the magnitude of this moment for me.

Fannar grinned. "I knew you'd love it. I have something to show you." He gestured for me to follow.

We wove through the labyrinth of shelves and ladders, our footsteps echoing softly. I counted maybe three students in the building. It was like the entire library had been reserved for us.

Fannar stopped abruptly, spreading his arms wide and announcing, "The astronomy section!"

A rush of giddy enthusiasm filled me as I took a few quick steps toward the books, celestial maps, and star charts. My heart leapt as I scanned the titles, recognizing some familiar names I'd only read about in the books that Fannar had borrowed for me. I reached for the nearest volume, eager to explore the cosmos through its pages, but Brontes caught my wrist gently.

"As much as I'd love to let you get lost in the stars, snowflake, remember why we're here," he said regretfully.

My excitement dimmed, but I nodded, backing away from the bookcase.

Brontes squeezed my shoulders into a quick hug. "We'll come back later, and you can read as much as you want."

"Really?" I asked, my eyes lifting up to meet his.

"I promise." He placed a soft kiss on my head.

"Okay," I agreed and turned back to Fannar. "Should we start with ancient history?"

Fannar nodded and steered us toward that section.

Once there, he stopped at a long study table that stretched across the aisle of bookshelves. The massive table of dark cherry wood, aged and weathered, proudly displayed scratches and wear indicative of its age. Eight matching wooden chairs with intricate carvings surrounded the table, while the warm light of desk lamps running along its center illuminated the scene.

"Let's set up camp here." Fannar tossed his backpack on the table.

"Okay," Helena said as the rest of us set our belongings down. "What's the game plan?"

"We should look for anything that might have information about Obsidia and her brooch," I said.

"Or even dark magic itself," Brontes suggested.

"Good point," Fannar agreed.

We all nodded and split up, each heading off into different aisles of ancient tomes that bore the weight of centuries within their bindings.

Trailing my fingers along the leather spines, I wound through imposing shelves that seemed to stretch on endlessly, heavy with crumbling leather tomes and fraying scrolls, and each one promising untold knowledge and wisdom. As I inhaled the earthy scent of ancient pages, the sheer volume of knowledge was dizzying. This place could hold the key to stopping Obsidia. All we had to do was find it.

We trudged back one by one, our arms laden with scrolls, tomes, books, or anything that looked promising. The dusty pages rustled as we began the tedious work of skimming every text for any mention of Obsidia, her brooch, or dark magic.

About two hours, Brontes suddenly caught my eye. Having finished his initial collection of books, he headed back to the table with another pile. But as he approached, it became painfully obvious that he'd miscalculated how many books he could carry. He struggled to maintain his balance as he wobbled toward me.

I rose from my chair. "Brontes, do you need help with those?"

"Of course not," he replied with a hint of playful arrogance in his voice. "I got this."

No sooner had the words left his lips than the unstable tower of books came crashing to the floor, sending a series of deafening thuds through the otherwise silent library.

Brontes's eyes widened, and he gazed at me with a sheepish grin. "Oops."

"I warned you." I smirked, shaking my head and trying to suppress my laughter. "Did you really need to carry all of those at once?"

"Alright, alright," Brontes mumbled with a soft smile.

I giggled as we bent down to gather the fallen books.

"I may have been a bit overzealous," he admitted.

Helena and Fannar chuckled as they headed over to help.

"Thanks, guys," Brontes said.

We brought them over to the table before settling down on our chairs again.

As we continued searching for clues, a feeling of warmth and fondness came over me as I thought about the strong bond we'd formed together. Apart from Fannar and I, most of us had only just met a few days ago.

Hours passed as we pored over countless scrolls and tomes. My eyes grew weary from squinting at the tiny script. A headache brewed behind my temples from breathing in all the dust and the scent of musty papers.

Just as the allure of dinner threatened the hope of finding anything useful, a fragment of parchment slipped from between the pages of a crumbling book. I cautiously unfurled the fragile, aged paper, expecting it to be another dead-end. My breath caught as I scanned the faded words.

"Guys, listen to this!" I said, my heart racing with excitement. "It's about the brooch." I read aloud from the page. "'Under the dark skies of a moonless night, an ancient and malevolent sorceress named Lady Calista sought the unparalleled power and strength of the gods. Utilizing the lost forbidden arts of Chaos Magic, she crafted a brooch of a black rose and imbued it with an arcane power never before seen by the Enchanted Realm. The brooch not only amplified the natural Enchanted powers of its wearer but also allowed them to wield Chaos Magic itself.'"

"Chaos Magic?" Helena cocked her head to one side.

"I've heard of it," Brontes said grimly. "But it's extinct."

"Not entirely, it seems." Fannar frowned. "If she can use Chaos Magic, it's no wonder why she could conquer the entire realm in other dimensions."

"Wait, there's more," I interjected and continued reading from the delicate, yellowed sheet of parchment. "'But a courageous group of Enchanted warriors united to confront Lady Calista and her ruinous power. They battled for three days and three nights, leaving the skies ablaze with the force of their magic. With the gods on their side, the warriors defeated the malevolent sorceress, shattering the brooch and ensuring its destructive power was buried forever. Today, we celebrate the one-hundredth anniversary of the day the Enchanted Realm was freed from the threat of the Black Rose Brooch.' This was dated over three-hundred years ago," I finished.

"So the brooch was destroyed more than four-hundred years ago?" Fannar pondered.

"Or so they thought," Helena retorted.

"How is that possible if Obsidia has it?" Brontes asked.

"Hang on." I paused thoughtfully. "According to this, the Black Rose Brooch was destroyed in our world . . . but what if the brooch in Obsidia's dimension remained intact? She just brought the one from her world into ours."

Helena nodded. "That would explain it."

"Then we need to finish what those warriors started," Fannar declared. "We have to find a way to destroy her version of the brooch."

"Do you remember that prophecy Obsidia mentioned?" I asked, trying to recall the exact words she said.

Brontes's eyes lit up. "Yes! She said that if she killed Gwyneira, the prophecy would never be fulfilled."

"When she attacked the Ice Castle, she said something else too." Helena furrowed her brow in concentration.

"Right, I remember that." Fannar tapped his fingers on his chin. "A storm of fire and ice."

"Hmmm . . ." I turned to Fannar and Helena. "Do you think they're the same or different prophecies?"

Helena shook her head. "No idea, but they must be connected somehow to what Obsidia has planned."

Brontes's gaze met mine. I saw the gears turning in his head. "If we can figure them out, they could be the keys to stopping Obsidia."

"Agreed." A fierce determination hardened Fannar's face. "We need to find out more about these prophecies."

Suddenly, my stomach rumbled loud enough for everyone to hear, rudely reminding me that we had skipped lunch. I glanced out the window. Dusk's fingers were already caressing the sky.

"But how about dinner, first?" Brontes put his arm around my shoulders with a wry smile.

Helena smiled. "Yeah, let's pick this up tomorrow. We got a lot done today."

CHAPTER EIGHT

HELENA

The musty scent of ancient pages tickled my nose as I trawled through another dusty book, the words about Enchanted *this* and magic *that* blurring together. Fannar, Gwyneira, and Brontes sat around the long study table, each reading their own thick volume on Enchanted history. We'd been cooped up for hours in the academy library, the four of us continuing our research from the previous day of scouring every document we could find about Obsidia and the prophesies.

After shutting book number twelve of the day, I rose from my chair to gather more when Gwyneira's soft voice caught me.

"Helena, I've been meaning to ask you something." She looked up at me with her pale blue eyes.

"What's up?" I asked, grateful for the break from page flipping.

"That wooden music box in your room," Gwyneira began, her face aglow with genuine admiration and fascination. Her body leaned toward me, as if she was drawn closer by her curiosity. "The workmanship on it is stunning. It's absolutely gorgeous!"

The image of the music box sitting atop my bedside table flashed through my mind. Its dark cherry-colored wood gleamed with intricate swirls etched around an ornate crest. The lid bore an artful carving of a volcano, which I'd found out from my roommate was the mark of a Fire Enchanted.

"Oh, thanks! It's pretty cool, isn't it?"

"Did someone give it to you when you arrived here?"

"No." I shook my head. "I've had it since I was a baby. It was a gift from my parents in the Unenchanted Realm."

"How is that possible?" Gwyneira's eyebrows furrowed, and she tilted her head, silver-blonde hair spilling over one shoulder. "It's clearly from the Fire Kingdom."

"How can you tell?" I asked. "I know it has a volcano on it, but I think that's just a coincidence."

"The crest that's on the sides of it. That's the royal crest of the Fire Kingdom."

"No way. Are you sure?" My interest was piqued. I leaned in closer, eyebrows raised.

"Yes, I've been studying the royal families of the kingdoms lately. I'd recognize it anywhere."

Before I could respond, Gwyneira called to Fannar, who was immersed in a heavy book further down the table. "Brother, why didn't you tell Helena that her music box has the Fire Kingdom's royal crest?"

"Uh . . ." Fannar's ice-blue eyes darted from Gwyneira to me and back again. "What royal crest?"

Gwyneira rolled her eyes. "Helena's music box on her nightstand has the Fire Kingdom's royal crest."

"It does?"

"C'mon, brother! You must've been in her room countless times."

"Never noticed a crest." Fannar shrugged. "I mean, Helena told me it was from her parents, but it's not like I sit there and study it."

I giggled as Gwyneira grew exasperated. Her eyes narrowed at him, and she shook her head.

"Ha!" Brontes's laugh reverberated through the library. "Yeah," he snickered, a mischievous glint in his eyes. "Clearly, he was distracted by other things while in Helena's room. Am I right?" he teased, bouncing his eyebrows suggestively at Fannar.

Fannar's pale cheeks flushed as Gwyneira let out an embarrassed squeak.

"Brontes, that's rude!" she scolded, her milky cheeks also flushing a light pink.

I shot Brontes a well-deserved glare, but I couldn't help chuckling a little. He wasn't wrong. Fannar and I had certainly been preoccupied with more pleasurable pursuits during his visits.

"Alright, alright," Brontes relented, holding up his hands in mock surrender.

As our laughter dimmed, Fannar said, "So back to this box. Why would Helena's music box have the Fire Kingdom's royal crest on it?"

"That's what we're trying to figure out," Gwyneira said, turning back to me. "Helena, can you ask your parents the next time you talk to them?"

Fannar gave me a sympathetic look. "They passed away."

"Oh, I'm so sorry," Gwyneira said softly.

"It's okay." I nodded appreciatively. "They died in a car accident when I was twelve. I went into foster care after that until I aged out of the system. I didn't even know I was Enchanted until I accidentally used my powers."

"Your parents never told you?" Brontes asked sadly. "That must've been frightening."

"No, they never said anything. I figured they either didn't know or planned to tell me when I got older but just never got the chance. The music box is the only thing I have left of them."

Fannar put his frosty hand over mine and gave it a supportive squeeze.

"You might be part of the Fire Kingdom's royal family," Gwyneira suggested.

"Obsidia did call you 'Fire Princess,'" Brontes reminded us.

She did call me "Fire Princess" . . . twice. I just assumed she had mistaken me for someone else. I mean, she was from another dimension after all. But why was the royal crest on my music box?

I blinked. An invisible weight pushed down on my skull, causing a dull throbbing in my temples. My blank gaze dropped to the ancient texts spread across the table.

Could I possibly be connected to the Fire Kingdom's royal family? If it was true, why didn't my parents tell me? Then again, they never told me I was a Fire Enchanted. No, me being royalty is absurd.

My parents were from the Unenchanted Realm. They must've gotten the music box from someone else. I was just a rare unicorn Enchanted that happened to be born to Unenchanted.

There must be some explanation for this, a simple mix-up or coincidence, right? How could I have grown up without knowing anything about this?

I chewed my lip, mind churning.

"Helena?" Fannar's concerned voice broke through my thoughts, his hand loosely shaking mine. "Are you okay?"

"I'm sorry, Helena." Gwyneira probably saw the shock written across my face, and her eyebrows knitted with worry. "I didn't mean to upset you."

"No, I'm fine," I reassured them, forcing a smile so they wouldn't worry. "It's just . . . a lot to take in."

"We'll get to the bottom of this." Fannar locked eyes with me, squeezing my hand again. "But for now, we shouldn't get ahead of ourselves before we have all the facts."

I nodded slowly.

"Alright," he said hesitantly, his piercing blue eyes searching my face for any sign of distress. "If you need anything, you know I'm here for you."

"We all are," Gwyneira nodded sympathetically.

"Thank you." I managed a small smile of gratitude.

The possibility that I could be related to the royal family stirred up emotions that I didn't expect. It had been so long since I'd had a family that I couldn't remember what it was like to be a part of one. But the more I thought about it, the more I started to notice a strange, empty void inside me that I hadn't realized existed until now.

Absurd or not, I needed to find out more about the Fire Kingdom's history, about its royal family. If there was even the slightest chance that I was connected to them, I had to know for sure.

My eyes scanned the various ancient texts laid out across the table in front of me before they fell upon a stack of books on the history of the Fire Kingdom.

I can multitask! I'll look for information about the royal family and the prophecies at the same time.

The others resumed their search for information on Obsidia and the prophecies. Fannar muttered under his breath as he poured through stacks of scrolls, while Gwyneira's fingers danced across the pages of countless volumes, making note of anything that might hold valuable insight. Brontes bustled back and forth from the table and shelves, replacing finished books with fresh ones.

I dove into the texts with renewed vigor. My eyes scanned the pages feverishly, hungrily devouring every bit of history they offered. Stories of fierce battles, great triumphs, and devastating betrayals filled the text, each one painting a vivid picture of the Fire Kingdom's tumultuous past.

The hours of research blurred together as a fortress of books surrounded me. My eyes ached from squinting at faded words, but I wouldn't stop until I uncovered the truth. The truth about my past, my connection to the Fire Kingdom, and my very identity were all tangled together in this mystery, waiting for me to unravel them.

Then, I finally found a section in a newer book about Fire Kingdom history, *The Last Fire Queen.* It told the tragic story of the Fire Kingdom's last royal family.

On her twenty-fifth birthday, Queen Scarlett ascended to the throne of the Fire Kingdom. She ruled alongside her husband, King Tindris, with a fierce determination to protect her people and provide them with a safe and prosperous future. Together, they bore two daughters, Aria and Helia.

However, in the same year that Helia was born, tragedy struck. An ambassador from the Ice Kingdom, seeking to sow discord, murdered the infant princess while visiting the Fire Castle. The Ice Kingdom refused to punish the ambassador, denying justice for the murdered princess.

Anger swelled within me, hot and suffocating. How could this have happened? The book gave no details on the crime itself, only that the Ice Ambassador had escaped to his homeland, never held accountable. It was maddening.

My heart ached at the thought of such an innocent life cut short. The murder of the Fire Princess and the lack of justice had caused the rift between the kingdoms, just like my roommate Iris told me months ago. No wonder

Fannar had been so reluctant to be seen with me when we first met.

Wait . . . I did the math in my head. Baby Helia was born the same year as me? My heart hammered in my chest as I flipped through more pages, eager to learn more about the royal family's history. Why was Queen Scarlett the *last* queen? I swallowed and read on.

As the Queen and King prepared the Fire Kingdom for potential war with the Ice Kingdom, a powerful and mysterious dark magic organization known as the Iron Circle invaded the Fire Castle in a surprise attack. King Tindris and his knights bravely fought to protect the royal family, but ultimately, the King lost his life in the battle.

Queen Scarlett and her eldest daughter, Aria, were never seen again. The Fire Kingdom was left to rebuild their kingdom, scared and grieving. The attack left the Fire Kingdom shattered, and it would take years to heal and recover under the governance of the Fire Council until the next monarch comes of age.

The rift between the Fire and Ice Kingdoms left a lasting impression on both kingdoms and still exists today. The fates of Queen Scarlett and Princess Aria also remain unknown.

"Shit," I whispered, my eyes widening with every word. The silence of the library seemed to amplify my racing thoughts. First, the baby was murdered. Then, the king. And the queen and princess were still missing.

How could so much suffering befall one family? My eyes filled with tears as an unexpected wave of emotion swept over me, overwhelming in its intensity.

My fingers traced the edge of the crisp page before turning it, revealing an image of a painting with such rich, vibrant colors that it seemed to leap from the book. It was a formal portrait of the royal family, depicted in happier times, their expressions serene and regal.

Queen Scarlett's fiery red hair cascaded down her back like a river of flame, her violet eyes piercing and powerful. King Tindris's strong jawline and perfectly styled black hair framed his striking green eyes.

My gaze shifted to the two-year-old Aria, her shoulder-length ebony hair like her father's and violet eyes so similar to her mother's. But it was Baby Helia who made me gasp—her few wisps of bright red hair and emerald-green eyes . . . just like mine.

My breath caught in my throat as my fingers left the page to grasp my own red hair. I stared at the face of the baby who could've been my twin. Baby Helia had been born the same year as me, sharing my crimson hair and emerald eyes. "Helia" sounded a lot like "Helena" too. This couldn't be a coincidence, could it?

Adorning the wall behind the family was a beautiful, ornate tapestry proudly embroidered with the royal crest—the same crest I recognized from my music box.

My heart ached and my hands trembled as I traced the portrait with tears streaming down my face. *Was this my . . . family?*

“Helena, are you crying?” Fannar rubbed my arm, concern evident in his voice.

“Look at this.” I gestured to the painting in the book, my hands still shaking. “What do you see?”

Fannar leaned closer, his brow furrowing as he studied the image. “The baby . . . She looks like you.” He looked back at me and then again at the portrait. “And so does the Queen, except for your eyes. Your eyes match the King’s.”

“Exactly! And the crest from my music box!”

“Babe,” Fannar whispered, placing a hand on my shoulder, “do you think . . . ?”

“I think I’m a fucking princess!”

CHAPTER NINE
HELENA

As Fannar and I sat in front of her enormous mahogany desk, it was strange to see how Headmaster Moira's office could remain spooky even with the midday sunlight streaming in. The book on Fire Kingdom history lay open to the image of the royal family, their faces eerily similar to my own. My wooden music box perched next to the book, emblazoned with the crest that matched the tapestry in the portrait.

Fannar held my hand tightly, his icy touch soothing the anxious heat within me. "It doesn't make any sense, Headmaster," he said. "Helena looks exactly like Baby Helia, along with her age and the crest. They can't *all* be a coincidence."

Headmaster Moira leaned forward in her chair, her eyes scanning my face, the book, and my music box. "I have to admit, the resemblance is uncanny." Her lips pursed to one side, as though she were piecing together a puzzle. "But Princess Helia was murdered as an infant."

"Was she though?" Fannar asked. "I've known the Ice Kingdom ambassador that was accused of her murder since I was a baby. Jokull is practically my grandfather. He always swore he didn't kill the princess. Could her death have been faked to hide her?"

"It's very possible." Headmaster Moira nodded slowly. "In fact, Queen Scarlett and the eldest princess, Aria, both survived."

"What?" I gasped. "But how? The book said they were still missing and presumed dead."

"That's what they believed at the time the book was written," Moira said gently. "But since then, there have been some developments regarding the Fire Kingdom's lost royals."

"Developments?" I asked urgently, desperate for more.

"Queen Scarlett and Princess Aria have been accounted for," Headmaster Moira began. "It turns out that Queen Scarlett escaped with Princess Aria to the Unenchanted Realm in order to hide from the Iron Circle. Tragically, the Queen passed away six years later, leaving Aria unaware of either of their identities until her powers manifested two years ago."

Grief and anger clawed at my heart as the loss of Queen Scarlett—my mother?—settled heavily upon me, mixing with a wave of relief knowing that at least Aria had survived. But the news left me reeling. I had a sister out there. I wasn't alone.

"The book said the Iron Circle used dark magic," Fannar recalled. "Could Obsidia be connected to the Iron Circle?"

"I doubt it," Headmaster Moira said thoughtfully. "I'm familiar with the type of dark magic used by the Iron Circle, and it sounds very different from how you describe Obsidia's magic. Also, Princess Aria defeated the Iron Circle in our realm shortly after she resurfaced here."

Aria had defeated the Iron Circle and avenged our family. My chest bloomed with pride for the sister I'd never met.

"Is Aria . . . Is she okay now?" I asked, not really sure why.

"From what I've heard, she's doing quite well." Headmaster Moira smiled softly. "The Princess currently attends Athenaeum Academy in Ravensbend—in her third year, by my calculations. She will ascend the throne of the Fire Kingdom upon graduation."

I stared at the portrait of the royal family again, my eyes tracing over the features of the baby princess that mirrored my own.

"Could I really be Princess Helia?" I whispered, almost to myself.

"I can't say for certain, but given Aria's history, it would be plausible for the Fire Kingdom to have hidden Princess Helia in the Unenchanted Realm as well."

"But, Headmaster, is there any way to confirm she's Princess Helia?" Fannar asked, his grip on my hand tightening.

Headmaster Moira pondered the question, her eyes narrowing in thought and then widening again as an idea came to her mind. "Perhaps there is something more we can do, Helena. With your willingness and a unique stone, I can create a portal that will allow us see into the past."

"Like my memories?"

"These may not be your own memories, but we will witness events that are connected to you, even those that you were too young to recall. The process can be emotionally overwhelming, but given what's at stake, it could potentially confirm your identity. I leave the decision up to you."

My stomach churned with anticipation, and I hesitated for a moment, locking eyes with Fannar. "What do you think, babe?"

"I think you know the answer, stubborn Fire Enchanted." Fannar chuckled softly. "You really think you can walk away without trying?"

The idea of uncovering secrets from the past was both exhilarating and petrifying. Once I walked through that door, there would be no going back. But all the strength I needed stood right next to me. My prince.

"Alright." I turned to the headmaster. "Let's do it."

"Very well." Headmaster Moira opened her desk drawer and retrieved a small stone. She paused for a moment to focus until the stone began to emit a soft green glow. Rising from her chair, she walked over and stood beside me. "Hold the stone in your hands and concentrate on your earliest memories. My powers will do the rest."

With a nod, I took the stone from her, its warmth pulsing against my skin.

She placed the tips of her fingers against one of my temples while her other hand pointed to a blank spot on the wall.

I closed my eyes and focused on my past, imagining myself as a baby and allowing the energy from the stone to flow through my arms and up into my mind.

A bright violet hue seeped through my eyelids, and I opened my eyes with a start. One of the headmaster's portals swirled open before me on the wall, but a kaleidoscope of light and color replaced the usual black center. I held my breath, transfixed, as the mesmerizing whirlpool of iridescent lights within began to coalesce, my memories playing out vividly before us like a movie.

There I was, a baby cradled in the arms of an older woman nestled together in the cozy cottage. Sunlight streamed in through the lace curtains.

"Hello, little one, it's Grandma. Did you have a nice nap?" my grandmother cooed, nuzzling my button nose as I left out a yawn. Her silver hair glowed in the warm light, falling around kind eyes and a face etched with laugh lines. "It's such a lovely day today. Maybe we should go take a walk with Grandpa later. What do you say, Grandpa?"

My grandfather, a tall man with gentle eyes and silver hair that framed a wise, weathered face, gazed down at me with pure adoration.

"There's my princess," he greeted. Grandpa's weathered hands engulfed mine, calloused thumbs gently stroking my tiny fingers. His beard tickled my cheek as he leaned down to plant a whiskery kiss.

I giggled and squirmed happily.

Grandpa chuckled. "How can you be so adorable, Helia?"

"She is precious, isn't she?" Grandma beamed, tenderly brushing her fingers across my chubby cheek.

"We'll need to ask your mommy to let us babysit you more often."

The warmth and security I felt in their presence enveloped me like a comforting blanket, their love for me filling the room with joy. A sweet melody drifted through the air, wafting from an intricately carved wooden music box that rested on a nearby table. I'd recognize the melody anywhere. It was my music box.

Suddenly, a series of loud bangs came from the front door. My grandparents' heads jerked up in surprise, shattering the tranquility of our moment together. Grandpa swung the door open, revealing a disheveled man gasping for breath. His once pristine uniform was tattered and smeared with soot and blood, the royal crest of the Fire Kingdom barely visible on his chest.

"Pire!" My grandfather instantly recognized him, his eyes widening with alarm. "What happened?"

"Your Highnesses." Pire collapsed to his knees, tears streaking through the grime on his face. "The Fire Castle . . . was attacked by the Iron Circle. His Majesty the King . . . is dead!"

Grandma gasped, her grip tightening as she clutched me protectively to her chest.

Grandpa was at the man's side in an instant, gripping his arms to hold him steady. "What of the Queen and Aria?"

"Queen Scarlett and Princess Aria . . . managed to escape," he replied through heavy pants. "They fled to the Unenchanted Realm. Her Highness Princess Helia . . . is now the last of the royal family . . . in the kingdom."

My grandparents exchanged horrified looks, and their gaze flitted back to me.

"They'll come for her next," Grandpa said grimly.

Grandma stifled a sob, face buried in my downy hair, kissing the top of my head. "We must protect her."

Baby Helia gurgled happily, oblivious to the peril closing in around her, but now as an adult, I could see the fear clawing its way onto their faces. Their eyes met again, both reflecting the same crushing realization—there would be no safe haven here for their beloved granddaughter. The Iron Circle would scorch the entire realm to find me.

The swirling mists of the portal shifted then, and a new scene unfolded. Night had fallen, and my grandmother stood next to a horse-drawn wagon filled with boxes and suitcases, tears streaming down her cheeks as she clutched a wrapped bundle tightly to her chest. My grandfather spoke in hushed tones to a couple, a younger versions of my parents—or who I had always thought were my parents.

"Take Helia to the Unenchanted Realm," my grandfather instructed them. "Find the Queen and give her this music box. It will prove the princess's identity."

"Please take care of her," my grandmother added, her voice thick with emotion.

My parents nodded. "Rest assured, Your Highnesses, we will protect her with our lives," Dad vowed solemnly.

"No one must know where, or even who, she is," Grandpa warned. "It's the only way to protect her from the Iron Circle."

"What about the people of the Fire Kingdom?" Mom asked. "Won't they wonder what happened to the Princess?"

"Yes, we will accuse the Ice Kingdom ambassador of murdering Princess Helia," Grandma said reluctantly, glancing at Grandpa. "The ambassador visited the Fire Castle just days ago. Our long-standing rivalry with their kingdom will make him the perfect target for our people's grief and anger. The Fire Kingdom will not question it."

"It is not ideal." Grandpa shook his head, his voice heavy with the burden of their decision. "But blaming the Ice Kingdom for Helia's murder will ensure her true whereabouts remain hidden from the Iron Circle."

He squeezed Grandma's shoulder. They each pressed a final kiss to my forehead and whispered words of love before entrusting me to my new guardians, bestowing upon them the responsibility of my protection.

With Dad at the reins and Mom holding me in her arms, the wagon departed into the forest. As my grandparents watched us disappear into the night, my heart ached from the immense loss for all of us, knowing I would never see them again.

The portal shimmered again, and a new view came into sight. I recognized the location as the apartment that I shared with my parents in the Unenchanted Realm. Laughter filled the air as five-year-old me ran into the living room, being chased by both of my parents—the Fire Enchanted couple who had sworn to protect me, their love and care evident in every touch and gentle word. A tearful smile spread across my face as I saw them once more.

"Got you!" Mom said as she snatched me up in a big hug.

I laughed and wriggled under her grasp. "No! I want to play again."

"Okay, one more time, and then we need to get ready for bed," Dad agreed. "Go hide and I'll count."

Once I had taken off again, Mom spoke in a low voice to Dad. "Any news about the Queen?"

"No," Dad sighed. "Even the private investigator has come up empty so far. It's like they vanished into thin air."

"I hope the Iron Circle didn't find them." Mom's eyebrows knitted with worry.

"Me too. Let's pray that Her Majesty is just really good at staying hidden. We won't give up."

"Right, nothing changes. We continue to raise Helena as our own daughter until we can reunite her with her family. We'll just keep searching, no matter how long it takes."

Dad nodded. "If we still can't find the Queen once Helena is older, we'll tell her the truth. Perhaps by then, it'll be safe enough for us to return to the Fire Kingdom."

Mom nodded with a sad smile.

"Are you even looking for me?!" I heard my younger version yell from another room.

Mom laughed. "We're trying, but you're so hard to find!"

"We're coming to get you!" Dad hollered.

As the two of them retreated into the hallway, the portal faded, and I found myself once more in the headmaster's office.

Of course, my parents never had a chance to tell me any of this or return to the Fire Kingdom. I was twelve when I buried them, victims of a senseless drunk-driver accident, before being placed into foster care. Suddenly alone in the world, I had wept until no more tears would come.

They had been the only parents I'd ever known. Through the years of laughter and tears, joy and heartbreak, they never once made me feel like I wasn't really their daughter, always reassuring me that I was loved. Despite the heartache and grief that clung to these memories, my heart filled with an overwhelming sense of gratitude, thankful for my grandparents and my adoptive parents who had all loved me so much.

The weight of my heritage pressed down on me, a heavy burden that both anchored and uplifted me at the same time. Tears streamed down my cheeks as I wept for the family I had lost, but also for my adopted parents who had sacrificed everything to keep me safe.

Fannar wrapped an arm around me, tucking me into his broad chest. "It's okay. I'm here for you, Helena."

His touch was soothing, like cool water on a fiery wound. I leaned into him, appreciating his support.

"Thank you, Fannar," I sniffled and wiped away my tears. "I just wish I could have had more time with them . . . all of them."

"I know," he said softly, rubbing my back in comforting circles. "But they loved you so much, and that's what's important. You'll always carry their love with you."

I nodded, taking comfort in his words.

"Now, we know you're really her." Fannar turned to Headmaster Moira. "She's Princess Helia."

Headmaster Moira nodded, a sad smile playing on her lips. "Indeed, it seems you are."

My gaze fell on the family portrait in the history book, at the tiny image of Baby Helia—me—still processing it all. "I just . . . I can't believe it. My whole life, I never knew who I really was. And now . . ."

Headmaster Moira gave an understanding smile. "It's a lot to take in, but at least you have the answers you sought." She rested her forearms on her desk. "I'm sure you know we will need to notify the Fire Kingdom Council of this news. They will no doubt be thrilled that *both* princesses have returned to the Enchanted Realm. But I will let them know that you will reach out when you're ready."

"Thank you, Headmaster," Fannar said, speaking for both of us as my mind reeled.

The melody of my music box filled Fannar's dorm room as we sat on his bed, the haunting tune a reminder of my newly discovered past. Fannar crouched down in front of me, taking hold of my hands on my lap.

"Helena?" he asked gently. "Are you okay?"

After a long moment, I swallowed. "I'm . . . not me."

Fannar frowned. "What do you mean? Of course, you're you."

"I'm not," I murmured. "Everything in my life wasn't what I thought it was . . . My parents weren't my parents. My home wasn't my home. My name isn't even Helena. I'm not who I thought I was."

Fannar shook his head. "That's not true." He stood up and sat next to me on the bed. "Yes, things happened in your past that you didn't know about, but your parents . . . They still raised you and loved you, didn't they?"

I nodded with a soft smile.

"It was still your home, even if it wasn't where you were born. Whether your name is Helia or Helena, *I* can tell you that you're still you."

He cupped my face in his hands, his glacial eyes *endless* as he gazed at me. "You're still that wonderful, beautiful, brave, and extremely stubborn Fire Enchanted I met, right?"

I chuckled weakly and nodded again.

"Well then, none of this changes who you are. So what if you're actually a princess? Royalty is overrated."

Just clinging to his hand, I smiled for a few moments. My Ice Prince, here with me. It didn't matter whether I was Princess Helia or Helena from the Unenchanted Realm—he'd still love me all the same. Having him next to me made everything less daunting.

My arms wrapped around his neck. "I love you, Fannar."

"I love you too." He kissed my forehead.

"Thank you for being here for me."

"Here for you?" He chuckled. "You're the one who's been here for me. After all I've put you through with my parents and my failed attempt at 'saving' my sister. I'm *lucky* you're still here."

I laughed back gently and gave him an extra squeeze. How could he possibly think he was the lucky one in our relationship, when he was the one who's had to put up with so much bullshit from *me?* But I suppose that was the wonder of our relationship. We *both* thought we were the lucky one to have each other.

My gaze fell on the music box again, the sound of its melody seeping deep into my bones.

"Fannar," I said and took a deep breath. "I need to go to the Fire Kingdom . . . to understand where I come from, and—" I hesitated. Could I dare hope that I would find my sister? That I could reunite with her as my grandparents and parents had always wanted?

"The Fire Kingdom? Now?" Fannar stiffened, his eyes clouding with concern. "Helena, I know you want to learn more about your family, but don't forget Obsidia is still out there. It's way too dangerous."

"Too dangerous for you, Gwyneira, and Brontes, but she doesn't care about me."

"You want to go without me?" Pain flashed across Fannar's face like I had just hit him.

I looked at him, my heart torn. "I don't *want* to go without you, but I know Obsidia wants to hurt Gwyneira the most. I would never ask you to leave her here." The strong pull I felt toward the Fire Kingdom was unmistakable—a need to reconnect with my roots and possibly my sister. "But I have to go," I insisted. "If they knew Helia is alive, it could heal the rift between our kingdoms."

"But you don't have to go *now*," Fannar argued.

"What if Aria can tell us how to fight dark magic like she did when she fought the Iron Circle?"

Fannar shook his head. "You don't know that Aria can help us."

"I have to at least try to find her." Frustration flared within me. "I need to do this, for myself and for the future of both our kingdoms. Don't you understand?"

A tense silence settled over us, the gravity of my decision hanging heavy in the air.

"I do," Fannar clenched his jaw, clearly struggling with his emotions. "But it doesn't make it any easier to let you go."

My anger evaporated. I took his hand.

"I don't like it," he mumbled gruffly. "But I know I can't stop you. If you really must go . . . just promise me you'll be careful."

My heart ached as I met his gaze. "I promise, Fannar."

He pulled me close and kissed me deeply, desperately, as if imprinting himself on me.

We stayed that way a long time, neither wanting to be the first to let go. But eventually we drew apart.

Fannar cupped my face in his hands. "No matter what happens, or how far apart we are, I will always love you. Remember that."

"I will," I whispered.

My journey to the Fire Kingdom was now inevitable. Despite knowing each step took me farther from Fannar, it was a path I had to travel to understand my past before I could build my future.

CHAPTER TEN

GWYNEIRA

My eyes flicked to Fannar again as I turned the page of another weathered book. His stoic façade, buried in his own book, couldn't hide the hurt that radiated from him. Helena's departure yesterday left a gaping wound, one I couldn't heal.

Despite Obsidia's desire to kill Fannar as well, I knew my brother remained at the academy because of me. If it weren't for me, he wouldn't hesitate to join Helena on her journey to the Fire Kingdom, even if it meant putting himself in danger. Although I never asked him to stay, I felt like a burden on him yet again for keeping them apart.

All the more reason to figure out how to defeat Obsidia as soon as possible. And the answers might lie in these timeworn tomes and scrolls.

C'mon, Gwyn. We need to find something useful!

I traced my fingers over faded glyphs and symbols, squinting at the tiny print in the light of the desk lamp. Then I saw it—a symbol I recognized from my studies.

Chaos.

Heart racing, I yanked a yellowed scroll from under a pile of scrolls, dust pluming, and unfurled it on the table. My eyes quickly skimmed the text.

"Brontes! Brother!" I cried, urgency coursing through me. "This is it! I think it's about Chaos Magic!"

Excitement bubbled inside me as I began to read aloud to Brontes and Fannar:

When Chaos unveils its shadow vast,

The realm shall tremble, futures recast.

From unity's heart, a storm of fire and ice shall rise,

Two become one, the key to the realm's reprise.

Powers merge, a hidden truth from the past,

For in combined might, the scales find balance at last.

"Well, that's not confusing or anything," Brontes said sarcastically, furrowing his brow.

Fannar smiled weakly. "You think they'd make it easy on us?"

"The first two lines 'When Chaos unveils its shadow vast, / The realm shall tremble, futures recast,'" I repeated. "That has to be Chaos Magic."

"'A storm of fire and ice,'" Fannar pointed out. "That's what Obsidia once said."

"But the rest of this . . . 'Scales find balance at last,'" Brontes muttered. "What does that mean?"

Fannar's gaze sharpened, his eyes flashing. "We should talk to Headmaster Moira. She can help us figure this out."

I nodded, gathering the scroll in my arms. Hope kindled within me like a flame. We had a lead at last, a chance to stop Obsidia's dark reign.

The three of us hurried through Haven Academy's hallowed halls, our footsteps echoing on the polished marble floors. I craned my neck, gazing upward in awe at the soaring arched ceilings painted with intricate murals and colorful stained glass depicting legendary figures and epic battles.

Like an ancient citadel, it radiated majesty with towering spires and sweeping staircases imbued with centuries of mystical history. I imagined what it would be like to have students brush past us in their vibrant uniforms, heading to classes on Enchanted Realm history, magical creatures, and advanced elemental mastery.

"You are so lucky to study in such a magnificent place, Fannar," I said as my cool breath mingled with the warm air.

"Yes, it's truly incredible, Gwyneira." Fannar nodded, his eyes filled with appreciation but also an underlying sadness that tugged at my heart. "But it's nothing compared to Brontes hiring the professors to teach you at the Storm Castle! Talk about pulling the king card."

"True." I smiled up at Brontes with my own gratitude, and he beamed back at me. "That's been pretty incredible too."

As we approached Headmaster Moira's office, a ball of nervousness fluttered in my stomach. Despite her eccentricity, I'd always admired her as the venerable guardian of this bastion of learning. Her wisdom and guidance had shaped generations of Enchanted from every kingdom. Not to mention, her status as the only Cosmic Enchanted in our realm made her privy to secrets most could only dream of. If anyone could help us unravel the mystery of defeating Obsidia, it was her.

The door to her office was opened, so Fannar poked his head into the doorway. "Headmaster Moira, may we come in?"

"Yes, come in," she called.

I followed Fannar and Brontes inside. The headmaster sat at her desk, her striking raven hair cascading over her shoulders like a glistening river in the moonlight.

"Ah, my young royals," she greeted us, her voice gentle yet commanding. "What brings you here?"

"Gwyneira, show her what you found," Brontes urged.

Hesitantly, I stepped out from behind the boys. The scroll crinkled under my fingers as I unrolled it across Headmaster Moira's desk.

"This prophecy," I said, my voice trembling slightly, "I-I think it's about Chaos Magic."

The headmaster's gaze sharpened as she peered at it behind her spectacles, scanning the text. "You're quite right, Gwyneira." She nodded thoughtfully. "It does appear to be related to Chaos Magic."

"But it's written like a damn riddle!" Brontes exclaimed out of frustration. "Every second this takes is another second that Gwyneira is in danger. We must hunt her down and end this!"

I laid a calming hand on his arm. Brontes was always so protective of me, but we couldn't rush into a battle with Obsidia blindly.

"Can you help us decipher its meaning?" Fannar asked.

"Let us examine it together," Headmaster Moira suggested, motioning for us to come closer.

Fannar, Brontes, and I leaned in, eyes dancing over the faded script as we studied the cryptic prophecy.

"So this first part: 'When Chaos unveils its shadow vast, / The realm shall tremble, futures recast,'" I read aloud, feeling the weight of the words settle upon us. "I think refers to Chaos Magic threatening the Enchanted Realm."

Headmaster Moira nodded in agreement.

"'From unity's heart, a storm of fire and ice shall rise,'" Brontes continued.

"Storm, fire, and ice," the headmaster mused, tapping her chin with one slender finger. "That could be the three of you and Helena. The four of you represent Storm, Fire, and Ice Enchanted."

My heart raced at the implications. Fannar, Brontes, and I glanced at each other in astonishment. *Could this prophecy really be about us?*

"'Two become one, the key to the realm's reprise.'" Fannar read the next line. "But who are the two?"

I pondered the question, biting my lip. A realization dawned on me. "Not who, but what. The next line starts with 'Powers merge.' Two powers become one." I jumped down to the last line. "Then, it says 'For in combined might . . .'"

"Like Combined Enchanted?" Brontes asked.

"Exactly!" I exclaimed.

"Yes," Headmaster Moira's eyes widened with excitement as well. "'The key to the realm's reprise' could mean that your Combined powers are the key to save the Enchanted Realm from Chaos Magic."

"'A hidden truth from the past . . .'" Fannar recited. "Do you think that's Helena?"

"Yes, finding out she's a princess." Brontes nodded.

"'For in combined might, the scales find balance at last,'" I read again.

"You must work together to unlock your full potential." Headmaster Moira pressed her hands together and touched them to her lips. "Your Combined Enchanted powers and unified strength are the keys to defeating Chaos Magic and restoring balance in the realm."

My heart pounded with exhilaration and fear, my mind racing, as she continued to speak, "The Chaos Magic that Obsidia wields draws its strength from disorder and imbalance. However, the four of you possess an incredibly rare trait—the ability to wield two types of elemental power in harmony as Combined Enchanted. Though you come from different kingdoms and backgrounds, by working together, you can create balance through your unity."

Brontes's handsome face hardened, and his dark navy eyes took on a steely glint. "We have the potential to stop her," he declared in a low, decisive rumble.

"Indeed, it is possible," Headmaster Moira agreed.

As Combined Enchanted, *we* were the keys to defeating Obsidia and protecting the Enchanted Realm. This was our purpose. Our destiny.

Fannar's face flickered with concern as he glanced at me. "But Gwyneira is the only one of us who knows how to control both of her powers."

"Then, each of you must learn." Headmaster Moira waved nonchalantly, as if accomplishing the task would be no trouble at all, her calm voice slicing through the charged atmosphere.

"Headmaster, how do we begin?" Brontes asked.

"You must train closely with each other and learn to work together in unison while mastering your dual powers. You must not only strengthen your skills but your bond with one another. Only then will you be ready to face Obsidia and the darkness that threatens our realm."

"Understood," Fannar nodded.

"Remember," Headmaster Moira cautioned. "In the face of chaos, unity and balance are your greatest weapons. Hold on to that, and you will prevail."

"Thank you, Headmaster." Fannar nodded with respect.

"Alright, we have a plan now," Brontes said, clenching his fists with renewed determination. "We'll train with our combined powers together. Let's start tomorrow morning. The sooner we get started, the better."

As we walked back to the dorms, Fannar's face grew grim. I could tell something was troubling him. I let Brontes know with a quick glance that we needed some space, and he adjusted his pace, lagging a few steps behind us.

"Brother, what is it?" I asked gently.

He paused for a moment before speaking. "Headmaster Moira stressed the importance of unity and training together, but Helena isn't even here." His brow furrowed with anxiety. "Without her, we don't have balance."

"She's only been gone a day." I gave him a comforting smile. "She will be back, brother."

He gave a heavy sigh. "I know she'll come back this time . . . but she's the princess of the Fire Kingdom. What if she decides her place is there, not the girlfriend of some prince from another kingdom? What if Helena doesn't come back to me?" His voice quivered with uncertainty as he voiced his fears aloud.

He looked away from me, his shoulders hunched forward as if he were bracing himself for heartbreak, and I realized this wasn't about training or Obsidia at all. The fear and insecurity that filled his eyes were about his future with Helena. My heart swelled with compassion for him.

"You can't predict the future," I said gently, "but one thing is certain. Helena loves you deeply, and nothing will ever change that."

Fannar smiled weakly at my words and gave me a small nod of acknowledgement.

I reached out and placed my hand on his arm reassuringly. "It'll be alright," I said softly. "Love always wins. You'll figure it out together."

Fannar let out a deep sigh before turning to me with a faint smile on his lips. "I hope so," he murmured.

CHAPTER ELEVEN

HELENA

Unicorn hooves clomped softly on the dark pathway. As the Ice carriage glided to a stop, I couldn't help but feel a pang of loneliness. I wished Fannar could be here with me.

Growing up an orphan, bouncing from one foster home to another, I had developed a fierce independence—something I prided myself in. Being alone was all I'd ever known, so why did I suddenly crave his presence so much?

Stepping out of the carriage, my boots crunched on the volcanic rock beneath them, and I took in the magnificence of the castle before me.

The bluish white hue of the carriage and unicorns stood in stark contrast against the looming Fire Castle, an imposing fortress of obsidian and basalt. A mixture of red and orange crystals embellished the surface and seemed to glow like embers in the sunlight. Jagged turrets pierced the smoky sky and glowing rivers of lava streamed down carvings of flames that etched down the exterior walls, creating an illusion that the entire castle was ablaze. It conveyed the intimidating power of the Storm Castle but with the artistic beauty of the Ice Castle.

Two Fire Kingdom guards escorted me through the massive ornate doors into a grand foyer. Our footsteps echoed as flames danced in elaborate sconces along the walls despite it being daytime.

They led me through the foyer and a series of long hallways. Exquisite tapestries depicting fiery battle scenes and spectacular sculptures of heroic figures lined the corridors. The air felt warmer than any other place I'd been, the scent of burning wood and spices filling my nostrils, providing a strangely comforting familiarity . . . yet still so foreign at the same time.

Eventually, we approached a set of ornate double doors. My heart thundered in my chest as the guards pushed them open, revealing a chamber with a semi-circle of regal men and women sitting on a raised dais. The Fire Council. In the center sat a middle-aged blond man.

My eyes immediately found Aria. She had been slouched in her chair like someone on their couch watching TV and only straightened up when we walked into the chambers.

Her long coal-black hair mirrored the portrait I'd seen of King Tindris, and her purple eyes matched Queen Scarlett's, but, most eerie of all, her facial features looked . . . a lot like mine. That was the uncanniest thing about the situation. A few days ago, I was an orphan, and suddenly, I had a sister who looked a lot like me. Aria grinned eagerly at me, and I smiled back.

"Welcome, Miss Helena," the lead member greeted, his voice warm yet cautious. "We are the Fire Council, stewards of the kingdom until our rightful heir, Princess Aria, comes of age."

His gaze drifted to Aria. Behind her stood a tall, toned young man with spiky blond hair and piercing blue eyes. His gaze followed me warily, intense and guarded.

"We've heard much about you," the man continued. "You claim to be the daughter of Queen Scarlett, Princess Helia, whom we believe is deceased."

Murmurs rippled through the council members, some hopeful, others skeptical. I made out a few whispers about having the queen's hair and the king's green eyes. The imposing spiky blond guy behind Aria crossed his arms, his eyes never leaving me, clearly unconvinced. His protective stance toward Aria tugged at my heart, reminding me of Fannar.

"Prove to us that you're Princess Helia," one of the council members demanded.

"Yes, anyone can claim to be her," another agreed. "Show us proof you are the Princess."

I froze, unsure of how to prove my identity. Then, I remembered the music box still safely tucked inside my bag. I pulled it out and carefully placed it on the table before them. "This music box bears the royal crest." I declared, hoping my voice didn't sound as shaky as I felt. "I've had it since I was a baby."

An elderly woman emerged from the back of the room. "Play it," she commanded, and I opened the music box as instructed.

As the melody began to play, Aria gasped, eyes filling with tears.

"That's my mom's lullaby," she choked out, her voice trembling with emotion. "She always hummed it to me before I went to sleep. I'd know it anywhere."

"As would I," the elderly woman said. She also began to cry. "For I was the one who imbued the magic into this music box. Its melody will only play when opened by someone of Fire Kingdom royal blood."

What the . . . ? It will? I never knew that.

A councilwoman stood up. "Let me try!"

Reluctantly, I closed my treasured music box and offered it to her. It was the only way that could prove my identity . . . but if she dropped it, I would absolutely murder her.

For a moment, doubt crept into my mind. What if the old woman was wrong, and it worked for anyone? I racked my brain trying to remember if I'd ever let anyone else open it before. I'd always been protective of it.

The councilwoman took it and carefully opened its lid. But, when she did, no sound came from within, to my own amazement and relief.

She returned the music box back to me, and I flipped the lid open. The gentle tune spread through the chambers once again.

Whew.

Astonished cries rose from the council, while others became tearful as the melody continued to fill the room. The leader held up his hand, motioning for silence.

"The music box confirms the truth," he declared. "Princess Helia has returned!" he exclaimed. "It seems *both* of our long-lost princesses have returned home at last."

The chamber filled with cheers.

"We have much to discuss, but you must be tired from your journey," he continued. "We will have maids escort you to your chambers, where you can rest. They'll make sure you have everything you need."

"No, allow me," Aria interjected. "I'll show my sister around."

"As you wish."

Once the meeting concluded, Aria rushed forward, throwing her arms around me. I froze, stunned by the embrace. Slowly, I returned it, tears springing to my eyes. A sudden warmth radiated between us, a connection I never knew existed.

"Helia," she whispered, and the sound of my birth name on her lips felt like a balm to my soul. "I can't believe I have a sister!"

"Neither can I!" I admitted, my voice cracking with emotion. We stood there for a moment, simply staring at each other, unsure of what to say or do. It was surreal, finally meeting my sister after all these years apart.

"Did you happen to bring Oreos?" Aria broke the silence first.

"What?" I said confused.

"Oreos. You're from the real world—I mean, Unenchanted Realm too, right? God, I miss Oreos."

I let out a loud laugh. "I miss Oreos too. And Snickers!"

"Yes, Snickers!"

As we giggled happily, I realized how similar the sound of our laughter seemed. It felt like a breath of fresh air having somebody from the Unenchanted Realm who I could relate to.

"I heard you went to Huttleston College before you got your powers," Aria continued.

I nodded. "That's right."

"I used to live twenty minutes away in Back Bay, trying to save up to go to Huttleston before I got my powers."

"Are you serious? That's crazy!"

"You remember that ice cream shop on Main Street?"

"Of course, they had the best salted caramel milkshake!"

"Yes, that one! I worked at the little convenience store next door." Aria rubbed her stomach as if she was hungry. "Oh, my God. I almost forgot about those salted caramel milkshakes. I would *kill* for one of those right now! So yummy."

We both broke out into laughter again.

I shook my head in disbelief. "All this time . . . we were only a few miles apart."

"Yeah, I know . . ." Aria said wistfully.

The spiky blond guy, who had been behind Aria, cleared his throat.

"Oh!" Aria gestured for him to come toward us. "This is my fiancé, Asher. His dad is the lead Fire Council member you spoke to."

Asher stepped forward and offered me his hand. "Welcome," he said solemnly. "I'm glad you found your way back to us."

My heart twinged as his icy blue eyes met mine, reminding me so much of Fannar.

"Thank you," I murmured. "It's nice to meet you."

He turned to Aria. "I'll let you two get reacquainted while I go talk to my father. Knowing him, he probably already has some celebration planned."

"Oh, that's totally unnecessary," I responded.

Asher shrugged. "There's no stopping him if he has an excuse to throw a party, but I'll try to make sure he doesn't get too carried away."

Aria nodded and smiled up at him. Asher gave her a kiss on the cheek. I could see their admiration as they looked at each other. They were clearly very much in love.

"Come on. I'll give you a tour of the castle." Aria's violet eyes twinkled before she linked her arm through mine. "We have so much to catch up on, so many lost years to make up for."

I nodded, overcome with emotion. "I want to know everything about you, about our family."

She led me into the grand main hall with towering ceilings and luminous chandeliers. Enormous floor-to-ceiling windows framed a breathtaking view of a majestic volcano towering in the distance behind the Fire Castle. A light-gray smoke billowed into the crisp blue sky with white puffy clouds. Rolling hills adorned the horizon, covered in lush greens and speckled with blooming wildflowers in shades of purple, white, and orange.

I gasped.

"What's wrong?" Aria asked with alarm.

"This is my painting!" I cried in disbelief, motioning to the volcano on the other side of the windows.

"Your painting?"

"Yes, I have it hanging in my dorm room. I always thought it was a mountain, but my roommate told me it was a volcano. It looks *exactly* like this."

"Really? Where did you get the painting from?"

"A friend made it for me, but it was based off drawings I drew over and over again with crayons as a kid." I took a deep breath. "I can't believe it was this place all along."

I often saw the volcano in my dreams, but now I wondered if those dreams had actually been memories buried deep inside me.

Aria smiled. "All this time, you never forgot our home."

I thought about that sentence for a long moment, and tears prickled my eyes.

Home.

And I'd been looking at it every day.

As we walked through the vast halls, our boisterous laughter echoed off the walls. Aria was almost as loud and obnoxious as I was—almost! I could already imagine Fannar calling the two of us "double trouble" when he'd see us together.

As Aria pointed out the finer details of the architecture, I marveled at the beauty of our surroundings, the rich tapestries and gleaming chandeliers. The scent of ash and fire enveloped me as we wandered the ancient castle. My fingers trailed along cold stone walls, tracing grooves and etchings older than memory.

Aria enthusiastically regaled me with tales of our parents, her memories of our mother's singing and our father's booming laugh. Her stories painted a vivid portrait of the family I'd lost, bringing them to life. We swapped notes of our similar experiences growing up in foster care and, eventually, discovering our fire abilities.

As we ventured deeper into the castle, Aria led me to an opulent sitting room, which was lushly decorated with thick carpets and ornate furniture. Luxurious curtains, draping to the floor, framed large windows, and warm light spread across the room from a multitude of dazzling jewel-toned lamps. A large portrait hung over a crackling fireplace with a gilded mantle.

I paused at the painting of a happy young family. A king, a queen, and their two daughters.

My family.

It was the portrait I'd seen in the Fire Kingdom history book that had set this whole journey in motion.

"Mother," I whispered. "Father."

"When I just need a break from everything else going on in the castle, I sit here and talk to them," Aria began hesitantly, her fingers lightly brushing over the golden royal crest embedded into the bottom of the picture frame. "Your music box . . . I still hum that melody to myself to remind me of Mom."

A lump formed in my throat. "I used to listen to it every night before bed. It was the only constant thing in my life."

Aria grasped my hand tightly, as though she could pass her memories directly to me through touch. Empathy filled her eyes. "Not anymore."

My vision blurred with tears. That music box had been my only comfort as a child, and now I understood why.

It reached across miles, realms, and even lifetimes to the mother I'd barely known and the sister I'd just met. The melody had been a thread connecting us all along.

I'd never truly been alone.

Together, as we stared up at the smiling faces in our family portrait, a missing piece of my soul clicked into place.

I was home.

CHAPTER TWELVE
GWYNEIRA

The hiss of lightning and sounds of ice shattering against wood echoed through the training gym, which was mostly deserted except for three other students at the far end of the building. Sunlight filtered through the high windows, casting long shadows across the floor. The air was heavy with exertion. Sweat glistened on our bodies as we relentlessly attacked the training targets.

Brontes, his body taut with concentration and his storm powers crackling around his hands, sent a bolt of lightning hurtling toward a target, smashing it to smoldering pieces.

I let loose a flurry of icy arrows, their heads honed to razor sharpness, and watched them sink deep into another target until it looked like a hedgehog stumbling out of a snowdrift.

Fannar tucked his chin and widened his stance, summoning a glacial wall between him and an impending volley of pretend fireballs. An onslaught of red paintballs burst against his icy shield.

On the surface, we formed a formidable trio, and training alongside my brother was another dream come true. But I knew this wasn't enough. Fannar hadn't summoned flames since the fall of the Ice Castle, and despite the intensity of our training sessions, Brontes's ice powers still hadn't manifested at all.

"Nice job, Gwyneira!" Brontes complimented, though his gaze flickered toward Fannar with concern.

"Thanks." I tried to sound upbeat, but my heart tightened as I watched Fannar as well.

He'd been struggling the last few hours. It was evident Helena's absence left more than just a void within our group. He hadn't been himself since she left.

"You got this, brother!" I cheered.

Fannar peered around the icy wall he had constructed, perusing an offensive path to take out the paintball launcher. He spotted an opening in the deluge of paintballs hurtling from the red-lacquered contraption. With a desperate lunge, he broke out of cover, attempting to dodge the shots, but he misjudged the timing.

My eyes squeezed shut as I flinched, only to hear the series of loud *thwap thwap thwap* sounds. When I reopened them, Fannar was covered with big splotches of vibrant red paint.

"Damn it," he muttered under his breath, disappointment cracking his usually stoic icy exterior as he slumped to the floor.

I exchanged a concerned glance with Brontes, silently acknowledging the strain on our team. How could we hope to reach our full potential when one of our own was drowning in pain and the other absent?

"Are you okay?" I knelt beside my brother, touching his shoulder.

"Yeah," Fannar replied a little too quickly. "Just a bit . . . off today."

"Maybe we should call it a day," Brontes suggested sympathetically.

"No," Fannar said firmly. "We can't afford to take it easy."

"Alright," Brontes sighed, looking unconvinced.

"Let's go again, then," I said, trying to infuse confidence into my voice.

Fannar nodded, his eyes hardening with determination. He steadied himself, focusing his energy on a new target. But instead of a precise strike, the icicles veered off in all directions.

"Gwyneira, watch out!" Brontes shouted just in time for me to dodge an errant spike of ice from Fannar. "Focus, Fannar! You almost hit Gwyneira!" he admonished.

"I'm sorry, sister," Fannar muttered, his eyes downcast. "I don't know what's wrong with me."

I know what's wrong with you, brother, but I can't fix it.

"Why don't we try something different?" I suggested, hoping a change in direction would help us regain some semblance of synergy. "Let's try combining our powers like we talked about earlier."

"Fine," Brontes agreed, looking at Fannar reluctantly.

Fannar nodded with clouded eyes, as if he wasn't fully present.

We took our positions, preparing to summon a harmonious display of ice and storm. I took a deep breath, my ice and storm powers thrumming within me. But as we unleashed our powers, the result was far from what we had intended. Jagged shards of ice and stray lightning bolts flew in all directions, crackling with dangerous energy. I had to duck twice.

Instead of a beautiful dance of ice and storm, the gym floor was marred with scorches and frost patches. Our movements, choreographed to be so perfectly synchronized, was in reality disjointed and faltering.

Fannar took another misstep that nearly caused Brontes to collide with him.

"Watch where you're going!" Brontes growled, his frustration simmering dangerously beneath the surface.

"Maybe if you weren't constantly in my way, I wouldn't have to," Fannar shot back, his voice tight with barely restrained anger.

"Guys, don't," I warned steadily but firmly, hoping to put an end to the hostilities. "We need to work together. We're all here for the same reason."

"Are we?" Brontes challenged, his piercing gaze pinned on Fannar. "Because it seems like someone's head is stuck in the clouds."

"Brontes," I scolded, though I couldn't deny my own growing concern for Fannar's state of mind. "We need to work together."

"Fine," Brontes huffed, his displeasure crackling in the air like a gathering storm.

We tried again, and once more our powers clashed instead of melding seamlessly together. The once pristine gym now resembled a battlefield, littered with icy debris and the acrid scent of scorched wood. My chest tightened with anxiety and ached for Fannar, but Brontes's patience evaporated.

"Damn it, Fannar!" Brontes snapped, finally losing his temper. "You need to get it together, or we're never going to get anywhere!"

"Maybe if you'd shut up, I could concentrate!" Fannar bit back, his eyes flashing with hurt and defiance.

"This is stupid. We can't keep doing this!" Brontes glared at me, waiting for me to step in.

"I'm trying my best!" Fannar's icy demeanor crumbling under the weight of his emotions. "Maybe it's not me! Maybe it's you!"

"Me?!" Brontes roared, his storm powers surging in response to his anger. "I'm not the one screwing up every damn exercise!"

"We just need more practice," I pleaded, hoping to diffuse the argument. "We need to do this together. Maybe it's a good idea for us to stop for the day."

My feeble attempt to quell the tension between Brontes and Fannar was in vain. Their voices continued to escalate into a shouting match, threatening to shatter the fragile bond that held us together. I finally had enough.

"Enough! Both of you, stop!" I cried out, my voice reverberating through the gym, drowning out the cacophony of their heated argument. "Headmaster Moira said we need to be united, not tearing each other apart. Remember why we're here."

My words hung heavily in the air, a stark reminder of what was at stake. If we couldn't find our harmony here, how could we hope to face the darkness that threatened the realm beyond these walls?

CHAPTER THIRTEEN

HELENA

The warm morning sunlight filtered through the atrium's stained glass, scattering colorful prismatic patterns on the marble floor beneath our feet. The scent of fresh coffee mingled with lavender and jasmine as Aria and I sat across from each other at a delicate wrought-iron table, sipping from our steaming mugs.

"Do you like your coffee extra hot too?" Aria asked unexpectedly.

"Huh?" I asked, my mind still aching from staying up into the wee hours of the night, talking with Aria about everything and nothing at all. "Actually, yeah. Fannar hates it!"

"Yeah, it's a Fire Enchanted thing." Aria nodded and then smirked over her mug.

"What?" I eyed her suspiciously.

"Oh, nothing," she said feigning innocence, but her violet eyes twinkled with mischief. "I just find it funny that a Fire Princess fell in love with—of all people—the Ice Prince!" She let out a loud laugh.

"It is funny, isn't it?" I smiled knowingly and took another sip. "Well, I didn't know he was the Ice Prince when I met him, and I definitely didn't know I was a Fire Princess until this week! But I'm glad you find my love life amusing." I winked.

Aria giggled. "I'm happy for you, little sis."

"Enough about my love life," I said, taking a sip of my coffee. The rich, bitter taste grounded me, and I let out a contented sigh. "There's something important I need to talk to you about."

Aria cocked her head in interest.

"Since the Fire Kingdom knows I'm not dead, they also know the ambassador of the Ice Kingdom didn't kill me. Do you think the Fire Council can mend things with the Ice Kingdom? It's important for our kingdoms to be on good terms . . . and, selfishly, it would also make things easier for my relationship with Fannar."

"Of course! You said the Ice Kingdom is still picking up the pieces from Obsidia's attack?"

"They are." I nodded.

"Once things have settled down for Fannar's parents, let me know, and I'll be happy to talk to the Fire Council.

We can set up a meeting between them and the Ice King and Queen."

"That would be great."

She reached across the table, grasping my hand firmly. "As future queen, I promise I'll do everything I can to keep peace between all our kingdoms."

I squeezed her hand gratefully.

Between Brontes, Gwyneira, Fannar, and me, we had the royals of three kingdoms in alliance. Not too shabby for the next generation of the Enchanted Realm, right? Now, if we could just survive Obsidia.

"Speaking of Obsidia," I leaned back in my seat, setting my cup down with a soft clink, "how did you defeat the Iron Circle and their dark magic? Any tips you can give me on fighting dark magic?"

Aria's face grew solemn, her eyes clouding over. "It wasn't easy. They were so strong." She paused, staring into her coffee mug as if reliving an unpleasant memory. After a moment, she met my gaze again, her voice steady and unwavering. "We were only able to beat them because of the Phoenix."

The Phoenix. I had read about it in the Fire Kingdom history book. It was an ancient force passed down through royal bloodlines. Aria and Asher were the bearers of the

Phoenix, divided between them in hopes of uniting their warring families against the Iron Circle.

"How does the Phoenix work?" I leaned forward, fascinated, wanting to know more about this incredible power.

Aria smiled softly, a faraway look in her eyes. "Asher and I both have the power of the Phoenix within us, but only half of it. We didn't realize it at first, but the Phoenix is symbiotically tied to our relationship. It draws its strength from our connection. Our love and our trust in one each other, not just physically, but emotionally too." Her eyes sparkled with awe and passion as she continued, "When those things are balanced between us, we can summon the Phoenix's full power together."

"Wow," I breathed, taking it all in.

So their victory had come not just from the strength of their powers, but from the depth of their bond.

"Love, trust, and balance," I repeated softly, allowing the words to sink further into me.

"Exactly." Aria nodded, a small frown forming on her lips. "I wish I had more advice to give you, but I'm not sure what else could help."

"Don't say that. This has been helpful already." I set my cup down on the wrought-iron table and grinned at her, my heart filled with gratitude. "I can't believe I'm getting advice from my wise older sister already!"

"I'm only two years older than you!" Aria playfully swatted the air. "You make me sound like an old man."

We giggled together.

Then, Aria's lips curved into a warm smile. "You know I'll always be here for you, no matter what. When you and your friends are ready to fight Obsidia, let me know. I'll be there. And Asher too, of course. Whatever you need, just as k."

Her support meant the world to me. After so many years of feeling alone, I finally had family again.

I reached out and grasped her hand. "And I'll be there for you too."

No sooner had the words left my lips than I heard soft footsteps approaching us. I turned to see an elderly woman entering the atrium. She walked with an air of grace that only came from years of wisdom, her silver hair framing her kind eyes.

Aria stood and gestured to the woman. "Helena, I'd like you to meet Etheri. She was our mother's trusted friend and royal mage."

"Your Royal Highnesses." Etheri inclined her head. "It's a pleasure to formally meet you, Princess Helia."

I blinked in surprise at the title but quickly recovered, dipping my head respectfully. "It's an honor. Thank you for helping me with the music box."

"You're very welcome, dear," she smiled, her eyes crinkling at the corners.

Aria regarded me curiously. "That reminds me, do you want to go by Helena or Helia now?"

I considered the question. Helia was my birth name, but Helena was what my friends always called me, the name I had grown up with in the Unenchanted Realm. Though I now understood my true heritage—that I was Princess Helia of the Fire Kingdom—I couldn't let go of the life I had known before.

My heart told me that it was important to hold on to both aspects of myself, the orphaned girl with newfound powers who had become a top ranking Fire Enchanted at Haven Academy and had fallen in love with the Ice Prince. "Helena" represented the life I'd built for myself beyond my royal blood.

"I prefer Helena with friends and family," I responded firmly. "But Helia can be my formal name for official royal stuff or whatever."

"Sure thing." Aria nodded in understanding. "You'll just be 'baby sis' to me, anyway."

I shook my head and chuckled.

"Your Royal Highnesses," Etheri began, "if you are done here, I have something for Princess Helia that I'd like to show her."

"Sure."

Aria and I followed Etheri out of the atrium down a long corridor adorned with murals that seemed to come alive as the flickering light from the torches danced across their surfaces. These images told the story of my ancestors, the great leaders and warriors who came before us.

My eyes scanned the scenes depicted on the walls, each one more captivating than the last, and Etheri noticed my interest.

"Your Royal Highness," Etheri said, her voice filled with reverence. "This is the bloodline of the Fire Kingdom. All of these murals, the artifacts, the portraits of heroes and kings, the very stones of this castle"—she swept her arm wide—"they're a part of you, Princess Helia. This is your history, your lineage."

Pride welled up inside me as we continued to walk through the corridor, knowing that I came from a long line of feisty royals and warriors.

Etheri led us to a large wooden door, and she pushed it open to reveal a small room filled with books, scrolls, and dusty artifacts.

"Wow," I breathed as Aria and I stepped inside. The scent of burning incense filled my nostrils.

Etheri rummaged the shelves lining the walls, filled with strange objects like colorful crystals that shimmered in the light, small potion bottles of various shapes, sizes, and colors with unknown liquids inside, and old spell books in leather with ornate designs. Scattered around the room were also carved stone figures, antique jewelry, and an assortment of mysterious trinkets that seemed to emit enchanting yet powerful auras.

"Cool, huh?" Aria grinned.

"Be careful not to touch anything," Etheri warned. "Some of these objects are more powerful than you can imagine."

I nodded, my heart racing with excitement. Some people referred to our powers as magic, but they were just our natural abilities. Etheri practiced real magic, and I had always been fascinated by the idea. This mysterious room was like a dream come true.

"Here it is," Etheri said as she reached into a small wooden box. She pulled out a stunning pendant of a phoenix, its golden feathers intricately crafted. "Your mother wanted you to have this when you came of age."

"Thank you," I whispered, my fingers tracing the metalwork.

"She wanted you to remind you," Etheri continued, her eyes locking onto mine, "that though you may not have the power of the actual Phoenix like your sister, never forget the spark that lives inside of you. This pendant signifies your royal lineage and serves as a token of protection."

When Etheri pressed the pendant into my palm, I knew she was entrusting me with more than an heirloom. She was passing a legacy to me. I may not have grown up a princess, but I would honor my mother's memory. I would make her proud.

"Etheri, tell us more about Mom," Aria pleaded.

"But you've already heard most of my stories, child," Etheri replied.

"I never grow tired of them. They make me feel closer to her."

"I would love to hear them," I agreed.

Etheri lowered herself into a chair, and we settled onto plush pillows on the floor. She began to share stories of our mother's valor, great power, compassion for her people, and the vision she held for a peaceful kingdom. I listened intently, my heart swelling with love and pride for the mother I barely knew.

My throat tightened. "I wish I'd known her."

"You both have your mother's spirit." Etheri's voice was soft, filled with reminiscence. "I can see her fire in you. To see her beloved daughters together in this castle again . . . She would have made been so proud."

As afternoon faded to dusk, each story filled a tiny piece of my heart that had been missing. The fuzzy image I clung to of my mother sharpened into someone real, flawed yet extraordinary. I could almost see my mother's fierce essence in the flickering flames of the candles that illuminated the room. She gave me a renewed determination to forge my own path while honoring her endearing memory.

Emerald and gold silk swirled around my legs as I swept out of my chambers, heels clicking on the marble floors. The gown clung to me like a second skin. I paused in front of an antique mirror, scarcely believing the regal woman in the reflection was me. The precious gems from the tiara on my head cast a magical hue around me. My heart raced with anticipation for the grand celebration ahead, the concept of being royalty still so foreign to me.

This is insane. My fingers skimmed over the cool stones.

A thousand past lives gazed down upon me as I walked through the portrait gallery of my ancestors. An overwhelming sense of familiarity and déjà vu filled my veins, as if I knew these people—my forefathers and foremothers—intimately, even though we had never met before.

Flickering firelight illuminated a particularly striking portrait of a couple. My pulse quickened as I drew closer until my breath caught in my throat. The woman had fiery red hair and stared back at me with bright green eyes. It was like peering into a crystal ball and seeing a future version of myself in ten years.

The portrait completely absorbed me, so much so that I didn't even notice Aria standing next to me until she spoke.

"It's uncanny, isn't it?" Aria gave a bittersweet smile. "You look just like her, Queen Liora, our grandmother."

An intricate gold embroidered phoenix adorned Aria's sleek crimson dress, a fitting tribute to the power living inside of her. The vibrant gown clung to her figure and shimmered elegantly in the light of the torches. Her usually straight black hair cascaded down her back in soft waves and a golden tiara of gleaming rubies sat atop her head.

"You were with her and King Axius when the castle was attacked," Aria continued. "They kept you safe from the Iron Circle."

I stared at the image again, my fingers itching to trace the lines of their faces. My heart ached that I never got a chance to know them or any of these people who had come before me.

But at the same time, I couldn't shake the nagging feeling that I didn't truly belong here.

My thoughts must have shown on my face because Aria reached out and squeezed my hand gently. "Hey, it's okay. You're still getting used to all of this, and that's perfectly normal."

"I just . . ." I shook my head, trying to find the right words. "I feel like I'm walking through someone else's life . . . like I'm an intruder in someone else's home."

"Helena, this castle, this kingdom, these halls are as much your home as mine now. You will always have a place here as princess of the Fire Kingdom. Whether it's on the weekends, during school breaks, or after we graduate, you can come home whenever you want."

"Really?" I asked, almost doubting that there was a place where I truly belonged.

"Of course! And when I'm queen, I hope you'll stand beside me and help lead our people," Aria declared, her eyes gleaming with determination. "Together, we have the power to make a difference in the lives of our kingdom."

The prospect of supporting my sister as queen filled me with a mixture of excitement and fear. But standing amidst the echoes of the past, a sense of awe and anticipation overwhelmed me as I realized all the boundless opportunities that lay ahead for my future. This castle of fire and ash, these ancient halls whispering of destiny—perhaps Aria was right. Perhaps this was where I belonged.

"Thanks, Aria. I appreciate it."

Aria smiled and linked her arm through mine. "Now, let's go party like a bunch of princesses!"

As we made our way to the grand ballroom, the doors opened into a sea of people, all dressed in their finest attire. The expansive hall was ablaze with light, laughter, and music as the feast to celebrate my return commenced. I was momentarily stunned by the opulent decorations and the pageantry. It was like stepping into a different world, full of glamour and extravagance.

"You have to go first," Aria whispered, squeezing my hand.

As the eldest and future queen, tradition dictated that Aria enter the hall last.

With a deep breath, I reluctantly released my sister's hand and descended the grand staircase into the crowded ballroom.

The herald's voice boomed out, "Her Royal Highness, Princess Helia!"

All around me, nobles and courtiers dressed in vivid silks and satins erupted in cheers and bowed deeply.

As I reached the bottom step, Asher's familiar smirk was a welcome relief.

"You're doing great," he whispered.

"Her Royal Highness, Crown Princess Aria. Future Queen of the Fire Kingdom!" the herald announced as Aria stood on the landing above the staircase.

The people knelt in a long, deep bow before exploding into another round of applause and cheers. Aria motioned for silence, and, almost instantly, the hall became deathly still.

"Friends and family of the Fire Kingdom, my heart is filled with joy as I stand before you tonight. Like the Phoenix raising from the ashes of death, Princess Helia has returned to us!" Aria gestured toward me, beaming.

The crowd erupted into cheers, and I couldn't help but smile back at her, feeling the bond between us.

Aria continued, "May we celebrate her safe return and the strength of our kingdom. Long live the Fire Kingdom!"

"Long live the Fire Kingdom!" the people chanted. "Long live Princess Helia! Long live Princess Aria!"

As the chants died down and the music resumed, the servants pulled open the towering doors to reveal a feast fit for royalty—succulent roasts, delicate pastries, exotic fruits. My stomach rumbled, reminding me I'd barely eaten all day.

As I took my seat at the head table, nobles approached bearing gifts of jewels, silks, and perfumes. "Welcome home, Your Highness," they murmured with reverence as they bowed.

I thanked them graciously, trying to mimic the poise Aria seemed to exude so naturally. Inside, I felt like a fraud. These people saw a princess, but I was still just Helena. I caught sight of my sister's encouraging smile, and Asher stood unwavering beside her, giving me a subtle nod. Their show of support steadied me.

As the night wore on, I found myself swept up in the festivities. Course after course arrived, the royal chef's mastery evident in each unique blend of flavors. My goblet remained full of the kingdom's finest wine. Musicians played lively tunes. All around me, conversation and laughter abounded. Growing up as an orphan, this was far beyond anything I had ever imagined.

Yet, despite the grandeur surrounding me, my thoughts kept drifting back to Fannar and how much I wished he were here to dance with me. How were Gwyneira and Brontes doing? Were they making progress on fighting Obsidia without me? Had she figured out they were at Haven Academy yet?

The ache in my chest grew heavier with each passing moment.

Later that evening, after the last song had faded, and the guests had gone home, I slipped away to my guest room. The beautiful space was adorned with rich tapestries and flickering candles, casting dancing shadows across the walls. The softness of the bed beckoned me, but I couldn't bring myself to rest just yet.

I paced the room, my heart and mind whirlwinds of emotion. Every second I'd spent in the Fire Castle had been magical, but I knew I was avoiding an important question: What did being the princess of the Fire Kingdom mean for my relationship with Fannar?

Aria was the future Fire Queen, and Fannar was the future Ice King. I couldn't be in two places at the same time. So if I truly belonged in the Fire Kingdom, did that mean I didn't belong with Fannar?

My mind raced as I forced myself to confront the agonizing decision—torn between my beloved sister and Fannar. It felt like my chest was being wrenched open from the inside, ripping my heart into two separate pieces that were devoted to each of them.

Where did I truly belong?

My thoughts turned to Aria and the sisterly bond that had grown between us. The connection we shared was undeniable, and I cherished the time we had spent together.

Closing my eyes, I imagined my sister as a queen. She sat next to Asher in the grand throne room, glittering crowns on both of their heads. I stood proudly next to them, consulting them on matters of the kingdom . . . but something didn't feel right. I felt happy for them, but not happy for me.

Disappointed in my own feelings, I opened my eyes.

What do ***you*** *want, Helena? No obligations. No pre-conceived plans.*

I closed my eyes again.

Imagine your future.

To my surprise, I found myself in the Ice Castle, frosty and unyielding. Yet, my heart felt strangely warm despite the chill in the air.

A cold hand reached for mine. It was Fannar. His gorgeous white hair flowed down his back, and he flashed one of his slight smiles at me. His icy blue gaze met mine.

The intensity of his stare made me feel weak in the knees, but it also filled me with a sense of comfort and belonging that I had never felt before.

"Fannar," I whispered, unable to articulate anything more.

Without a word, he pulled me into his embrace, his strong arms wrapping around me and his body radiating a coldness that felt exhilarating. My heart raced as I melted into him, his breath on my neck as he leaned in closer, his lips brushing against my skin. This was where I belonged. In his arms.

That's when I knew.

My eyes flew open, a sudden clarity washing over me. I finally allowed myself to sink into the luxurious bed. I drifted off to sleep, knowing with absolute certainty where my heart truly belonged.

Though Fannar and I didn't have an all-powerful force split between us like Aria and Asher, he was my balance, my other half.

The Fire Kingdom may be my past, my birthright, my home—but my future wasn't here. It was wherever Fannar was.

CHAPTER FOURTEEN
GWYNEIRA

Brontes and Fannar were at it again. Their voices grated like steel off the gym walls. As another quarrel flared between them, I watched on with a silent sigh.

The bickering showed no signs of cooling. Their tempers were more becoming of petty boys than the nobles they truly were. At that point, I abandoned my attempts to intervene. Gathering my belongings, my cheeks burned with frustration. Perhaps a nice lunch would soothe my rattled nerves.

Just as Brontes was about to deliver another retort, Fannar's head snapped around with lightning speed, like a compass pointing north to its destination. His attention completely focused on the gym doors, as though he could sense a sudden shift in energy before he even saw her.

The doors flew open, slamming against the walls with a resounding crash, and a familiar, boisterous voice echoed through the gym, causing my heart to leap in my chest. "You guys miss me?"

Helena sauntered into the gym, her wildly red hair bouncing in waves around her shoulders and her green eyes sparkling with enthusiasm.

"Helena!" I exclaimed, breaking through the previous tension between Brontes and Fannar.

The sight of her brought a surge of relief, joy, and intrigue all at once. How did her trip to the Fire Kingdom go? Did she meet her sister? Did she resolve the bad blood the Fire Kingdom had for the Ice Kingdom? My mind raced with questions, but I was content to let them swirl unanswered for now.

"About time you showed up," Brontes grumbled, though his hostile expression softened.

"I see you had a fight with the fireball launcher, babe," Helena quipped at the sight of Fannar covered in red paint splatter.

My brother didn't respond. His eyes met Helena's, and the air grew eerily still, as if the world seemed to hold its breath. As their gazes locked, a torrent of emotions flowed through them in a silent conversation that only they could understand.

My heart pounded in my ears as we waited for one of them to speak. But no words came, and the silence stretched on. The future of our team hung in the balance, and the gravity of our destiny suddenly felt heavier than ever before.

Once Helena returned, we took a break from training and enjoyed lunch together. She shared her adventures in the Fire Kingdom with us, and we told her about Headmaster Moira's theory that our Combined Enchanted abilities could be instrumental in defeating Obsidia.

"So what now?" I asked.

"We have to train hard," Brontes answered firmly. "All of us must gain control over our secondary powers so we can reach our full potential. Assuming we can do that, we can come up with a strategy to fight Obsidia that takes advantage of all our powers."

"You know how to do that?" Helena asked.

Brontes nodded. "My father always insisted on teaching me as much military history as he could. I can finally put all those hours to use."

"But the three of us have been training for three days now," Fannar reminded. "You and I aren't even close to summoning our secondary powers."

"Perhaps we've been approaching this all wrong," Brontes said thoughtfully. "True, we've been training together, hoping the powers would appear on their own, but we haven't stopped and just learned how to summon them."

"Learn from who?" Helena chimed in.

Brontes motioned toward me. "Gwyneira could teach us."

I stiffened suddenly. "Me? Really?"

"You're the most adept of all of us. And you might end up being the crux of the plan."

"How could *I* possibly be the most adept of us?" I stared at him in disbelief.

"You're the only one who can control both of their powers," Brontes pointed out. "Helena and I can't summon ice yet. Fannar hasn't been able use fire again since the Ice Kingdom attack. You're the only one of us who can do both easily. Not to mention, you knew how to use them skillfully enough to defeat my parents! That might make you the main attacker in our plan."

I . . . am the strongest of us all? Even stronger than Helena? Even stronger than my brother?

"That's right." Fannar's eyes widened, recalling the story we had told him when we first reunited. "How did you learn how to use your powers, sister?"

Suddenly, both Fannar and Helena looked at me—at *me*—with riveting awe, filling my chest with a warmth that rose to my cheeks. I'd always been talked down to, dismissed. Having people I admired look to me for answers was completely new.

"Oh . . . well," I stammered, "the servants at the Storm Castle used to play games with their powers . . . and they wanted me to play, so . . . well, I just played with them."

Fannar's mouth hung open in a shocked expression, his eyes stared at me in disbelief. He appeared astonished, unable to process what I had just said. His posture was as still as a statue as he stared at me with an intense gaze. "And you learned how to use your powers just like that?"

"Uh . . . yes." I shot a quick, anxious look at my brother and saw that he still seemed thoroughly bewildered. "Sorry," I said, purely out of instinct.

"Don't apologize! I'm so proud of you," he beamed, placing his hand on my shoulder.

I stood in shock as my brother's words sunk in. He was proud of me. His eyes glowed with admiration, and his smile stretched from ear to ear. My heart swelled with indescribable joy. Tears pooled in my eyes as I tried to swallow past the lump of emotion in my throat.

As I stood frozen, Brontes smiled softly, knowing how much this moment with my brother meant to me. "Gwyneira, you're stronger than you believe you are. So, will you teach us?"

I hesitated for another moment before nodding. "I've never taught anyone how to do anything before, but I'll do my best."

"Good." Brontes nodded. "So I think that learning ice would be the smartest option for us right now, since it's the one element that we all share."

"Sounds good. I don't even know where to begin with ice." Helena giggled.

"Neither do I." Brontes chuckled lightly. "Depending on how this goes, Fannar and I can come up with our battle plan."

Fannar nodded firmly.

"Great!" Helena crowed. "Let's get to it!"

CHAPTER FIFTEEN
HELENA

"Summoning ice takes inner calm," Gwyneira said, her soft voice floating through the gym. "No strong feelings, only tranquil stillness."

She inhaled deeply, her delicate features smoothing into neutrality. With a graceful sweep outward, her hands summoned a glossy sheet of ice across the floor.

"Now you try," she encouraged.

Fannar kept his distance across the gym, pummeling a punching bag with icy shards that glinted under the harsh lights. The rhythmic thud of his blows set an urgent tempo.

"How'd you make it snow before?" Brontes asked eagerly, leaning toward Gwyneira. "I gotta try that!"

She giggled, the sound high and melodic. "Baby steps first! Just the basics."

Brontes scoffed good-naturedly, his dark eyes glinting with humor.

“Eyes closed now,” Gwyneira instructed gently. I let my lids sink shut, enveloping me in darkness.

“Clear everything from your mind,” she continued, her voice floating disembodied in the void.

Easier said than done. Stray thoughts kept invading the forced calm.

Am I doing this right?

I feel like an idiot just standing here . . .

I gritted my teeth, trying to force the disruptive thoughts into submission through sheer willpower. A vein in my temple throbbed from the effort.

“When your mind is empty, summon your power and release it!” Gwyneira directed.

I flung my hands outward, eyes flying open. But only dissipating smoke curled from my palms.

Brontes extended his muscular arm tentatively. No ice crystallized, but sparks of azure lightning crackled from his fingertips, leaving the faint odor of ozone hanging in the air.

“That’s not right.” He frowned, knitting his dark brows together. “Any other tips?” he asked.

Gwyneira chewed her lower lip, wringing her slender hands in frustration. I felt a pang of sympathy for her. She so clearly wanted to guide us through summoning our powers.

"What else do you do to summon ice?" Brontes prodded gently.

Gwyneira's skinny shoulders hunched inward, her fingers twisting faster as color rose to her pale cheeks.

"Let's try again," Brontes suggested, his deep voice coaxing. "We'll get this."

I nodded firmly, rolling my shoulders back. "Yeah, we got this."

As I closed my eyes once more, I wrestled to suppress the stampede of thoughts battering my mind through sheer stubbornness. But an undercurrent of anxiety still pulsed through me as I released my power.

Fiery heat erupted from my palms. "Shit," I muttered.

Gwyneira studied the scorched floor, crestfallen.

"This is way harder than I thought," she said softly. Forcing a faint smile, she added, "Let me talk to Fannar."

"We'll keep practicing," Brontes said, his deep voice echoing through the gym. "Hopefully, we'll get the hang of it."

As she trotted off, Brontes closed his eyes and held out his hands, brow furrowed in concentration. I followed suit, letting my eyelids fall shut.

Calm thoughts, calm thoughts . . .

But my mind buzzed like a frantic beehive. Clearing it was easier said than done.

A sharp zap jolted through me, and I flinched, biting back a yelp.

Does ice feel like that?

"Damn," Brontes muttered.

I kept my eyes squeezed shut, sensing another electric spark flying my way. At the last moment I snapped them open, just in time to see it sail past my shoulder.

"Hey, watch it with the sparks!" I said.

"Oh, my bad," Brontes replied, looking sheepish.

He closed his eyes again, electricity already crackling at his fingertips. I tensed, waiting for the inevitable.

Zap!

A spark hit my side, stinging through my shirt. "Ow! Knock it off, man!"

I flicked my wrist, sending a whip of flame to singe his calf. Brontes's eyes flew open.

"What the hell?!"

"I said stop zapping me!"

"It's not on purpose!" he argued.

I swept my arm, shooting more flames at his feet. Brontes yelped and leapt away.

"Whoopsie, hand slipped," I sneered.

Pain sliced up my arm as one of his lightning bolts struck it, muscles seizing.

"Whoops, my bad," Brontes shot back mockingly.

We both dissolved into laughter, the sound echoing off the gym walls.

"Oh, you wanna go, Storm Boy?" I taunted.

I unleashed a blazing wave of fire across the hardwood floor. But suddenly Brontes was gone, encased in a small swirling tornado as he rose into the air.

"Hey, no fair!" I called up to him. "I thought you had lightning, not wind!"

A dark thundercloud formed over my head. Brontes's delighted cackle ringed from within the tornado. Jagged lightning bolts crashed down around me, and I danced wildly to avoid the sparks.

Time to take this up a notch.

I aimed a fiery blast beneath my feet, rocketing up through the belly of the cloud until I emerged face-to-face with Brontes. His navy blue eyes widened in surprise before I lobbed a fireball at his head.

He dissolved the tornado, dropping into a graceless sprawl on the gym floor. As Brontes scrambled up, eyes narrowed, I followed him down, pelting him with fireballs that he barely managed to dodge.

Landing in a crouch, I swept my gaze left and right looking for Brontes. A swirling tornado barreling my way was the only warning before it slammed me backward across the hardwood.

"Shit!" I yelped.

Before I could hit the far wall, a pair of cold, strong arms caught me. I looked up into Fannar's amused icy blue eyes.

"Language," he gently mocked.

"Thanks, babe!" I smiled at him.

I laughed sheepishly as Brontes approached. The fight had ended, but the fun had just begun.

"Shall we call that a win for me?" Brontes asked, grinning.

I stood, cracking my knuckles. "No way. You only won because you caught me off guard. Round two, let's go!"

Fannar chuckled. "Weren't you supposed to be learning how to use ice?"

"We're just blowing off some steam," I said with a casual shrug. Though his smile didn't reach his eyes.

"I don't know how you two can be so relaxed with Obsidia looming over us."

Brontes trotted over. "Sometimes fun is what unlocks our potential. Right, Gwyneira?"

She nodded, peeking out from behind Fannar.

"Come spar with us," Brontes invited Fannar.

Fannar started to decline, but a spark from Brontes zapped his thigh.

"*Hey!*" Fannar yelped, startled.

I knew it hadn't really hurt him. We just wanted to draw him in.

"Not funny!" Fannar protested as I flicked a coil of fire at his hand.

He recoiled. "You too, Helena?"

"Show us some fire!" I teased.

Another spark hit his backside. "*Gwyneira!*"

She smiled impishly as I cackled. My flickering flame made her shriek and duck. But then she returned a tiny shock of her own, making me yelp playfully.

Soon sparks flew as Brontes and Gwyneira ganged up on me. I unleashed ribbons of fire, dodging their lightning bolts.

"Help me, two against one!" I called to Fannar.

He hesitated. "I can't just—"

"Don't think, just do it!"

Fannar's face hardened with determination as stray bolts hit him. I could see him reaching his limit.

"Use your fire!" I pushed.

A bolt narrowly missed his face. Fannar thrust his palms out, flame erupting forth.

We froze in awe. Then I whooped, "Yeah! Go Team Fire!"

Laughter filled the gym as we resumed sparring wildly. Adrenaline pumped through my veins. We battled until, one by one, we collapsed in exhausted heaps.

I sprawled across Fannar's lap, looping my arms around his neck. "You're so warm," I murmured.

He laughed, the sound rumbling through his chest. "I feel it."

I nestled against him. "I'm proud of you."

Fannar smiled, leaning his head atop mine. "Now we just need to teach you ice."

The silence between us hung heavily in Fannar's dorm room as we got ready for bed. I busied my hands brushing my hair, stealing furtive glances at Fannar. He sat on the edge of his bed, his broad shoulders uncharacteristically slumped, and his arctic eyes carried a distant glaze as he stared vacantly into the nothingness of the floor, sending a pang through my chest.

Things had been strange between us since I returned from the Fire Kingdom earlier today, as if an impenetrable awkwardness had wedged itself between us.

He had withdrawn into himself, and it felt like he was pulling away from me, from us. My stomach twisted uneasily. After everything we'd been through, were we really drifting apart so quickly? I knew I needed to say something, to clear the unspoken words hanging in the air, but part of me hesitated, afraid of what he might say.

After what felt like an eternity, I took a deep breath, finally steeling my nerve to cut through the stillness. It was now or never.

"Fannar?" I asked tentatively.

"Hmm?" His pale blue eyes met my gaze.

"Is everything okay between us?" My voice came out shakier than I intended.

He looked up at me, surprise flickering across his face. "Of course. Why do you ask?"

Fidgeting with the hairbrush in my hands didn't offer much to calm my nerves as I attempted to build up the courage to continue. "You've been acting strange since I came back. You've been so . . . distant. Are you mad at me?"

Fannar sighed, running a hand through his white-blond hair. "No, of course not. I'm not mad at you, Helena. I just . . . I want to give you space to figure things out."

Stepping forward, I moved closer, hovering in front of him as I searched his face. "Figure what out?"

"Your future. Your sister offered you a home and an important role in the Fire Kingdom. That's huge." He turned away. “You have a lot to think about, and I don’t want to get in the way of that.”

My heart dropped into my stomach. Did he not want to be together anymore because I was the Fire Princess?

Fannar continued, his voice now tinged with vulnerability. “You’ve discovered a whole new part of yourself that you’ve never known. I want to you to have space to figure out your future as the Fire Princess and what you want . . . without any obligations to me.” He met my gaze again, ice-blue eyes glistening. “But I can’t lie and say I’m not scared of losing you.”

“Fannar . . .” I sat down beside him on the bed, taking his hands in mine.

“No, let me finish,” he hushed. “I’m terrified that your destiny might take you from me. I can’t bear the thought of losing you. But, more than anyone, I understand having a duty to your kingdom. So, if you must go . . .”

As Fannar’s confession trailed off, fear and vulnerability shone in his icy eyes. I knew how hard that was for him to say. My breath caught in my throat as understanding dawned on me. He was worried I’d choose the Fire Kingdom over him, over us, and he was willing to let me go if that’s what I wanted. But it wasn’t.

“Fannar, listen. You are what I want. I’m thrilled that I have a sister and a place in the Fire Kingdom, but it could never replace what we have." I squeezed his hands, urging him to feel the truth of my words. "You are my destiny. My future is with you."

Relief flashed across his face. His arms wrapped tightly around me, as if he was afraid I would slip away. I buried my face in his chest, breathing in his familiar scent of pine and snow. The steady beat of his heart soothed my own.

"Though I do have one request," I quipped with a grin. "Can you please have your parents put in heaters when they rebuild the Ice Castle? At least in some of the rooms?"

He chuckled, pulling back just enough to meet my eyes. The warmth and affection shining back at me chased away the last lingering chill between us. Fannar's fingers brushed my cheek, and I leaned into his touch.

"I missed you," he murmured, flashing his gorgeous smile.

"I missed you too," I whispered.

His arctic eyes softened. Slowly, he leaned in and pressed his lips to mine. The familiar cool thrill rushed through me. No matter how many times we kissed, it never got old.

My fingers twisted into his soft white hair as the kiss deepened. His strong arms wrapped around my waist, eliminating any space left between us. I melted against his muscular frame, my body molding to his.

When we finally pulled apart, breathless, Fannar rested his forehead against mine. His muscles relaxed as the last of his tension melted away. We stayed that way for a long time. No more words needed to be said.

For a few moments, all the turmoil, uncertainty, and anxiety over the fate of the Enchanted Realm faded away as we stayed locked in our embrace. Everything felt right again. I found my home, my purpose—right here in his arms. We had each other. That was all that mattered.

CHAPTER SIXTEEN
GWYNEIRA

The moment I awoke the next morning, I laid in Helena's bed in her dormitory room, wracking my brain on how to explain ice powers to Helena and Brontes. Our playful spar had been a brilliant idea, finally making Fannar comfortable with his secondary fire abilities. But it highlighted the unveiled differences I struggled to articulate between passionate and tranquil elements.

I couldn't fail at teaching the others, not so soon after they'd entrusted me with this responsibility. The expectation pressed heavily on my slim shoulders. I'd agonized over it during my sleepless night, mind racing to find the right words.

Brontes awoke with a loud yawn. He must've seen my fatigue. His strong arms wrapped around me, pulling my back tightly against his muscular chest. Warm lips grazed my neck tenderly, drifting up to nuzzle my ear. I exhaled, melting into his reassuring strength. With

Brontes's support, I would find a way to guide our friends. Failure was not an option.

"Good morning, my queen," he murmured, voice still husky with sleep.

My heart fluttered at his words, and heat rushed to my cheeks as it always did when he used that affectionate title. I couldn't restrain a giggle. "Good morning, my king!"

"Did you sleep well?"

I hesitated, fidgeting with the edge of the blanket. "Well . . . uh . . ."

"So that's a no," Brontes concluded calmly. He pressed a kiss to the top of my head. "What's wrong, snowflake?"

I sighed, the sound small and defeated. "I just don't know how to teach you and Helena how to use your ice powers. You said it's key for our battle plan."

"It is, but don't worry about it. We're Combined Enchanted, born to wield different elements. We'll figure it out together."

I nibbled my lip anxiously. "I know, but . . . you all trusted me with teaching you, and I'm failing already."

"Hey, no way." He gave me a sympathetic glance. "Let's try again right now. You and me."

Gentle hands gripped my shoulders, coaxing me to roll over and face him. I drank in the sight of his handsome features, all chiseled lines and artistic angles.

His wavy black hair was endearingly mussed from sleep. Temporarily dazzled, I almost forgot our conversation.

"Teach me," he prompted.

I blinked. "Huh?"

"How do you summon ice? Don't overthink it. Just talk me through it." His navy eyes bored into mine intently.

"Um . . ." I still struggled to verbalize the instinctive process. "Summoning ice requires pushing feelings aside to focus solely on the task at hand," I explained slowly. "Don't dwell on emotions. Concentrate entirely on what needs to be done in that moment."

Brontes nodded, his brow furrowed in concentration. "Right, you said we need a blank mind to wield ice magic."

"Not exactly blank," I clarified. "Thoughts will still come. Simply acknowledge then release them. Don't cling to anything except your purpose." I hoped my guidance was clear enough.

"Release my thoughts," Brontes murmured. His gaze grew distant, turned inward.

Abruptly he sat up, eyeing a vase on the windowsill. "No emotions," he repeated under his breath. Eyes closed, Brontes extended his palm. Nothing happened. Shoulders slumping, he sighed, "Damn."

I hesitated before gently asking, "Is there anything that makes you feel numb?"

Brontes thought a moment before giving a hollow chuckle. "Listening to my father drone on about military strategy usually did the trick. I was bored to death."

"Okay, imagine that." I giggled. "Now, give it another try."

Brontes's eyes closed, and his handsome features smoothed into an emotionless mask. He raised his hand once more. This time, frost crept steadily across the vase's surface.

"My gods!" I cried joyfully. "You did it!"

"Did I?" Brontes stared at the icy vase and back at his hands. He lifted them again to conjure a cluster of snowflakes that danced around us. He grinned at me, his boyish delight melting my heart. "Thanks to a certain gifted teacher."

Suddenly, a jolt of cold shot through my fingers and frost bloomed between our palms, sealing them together in an icy grip. We gaped at our clasped hands, stunned by this new development.

"Oh no!" I gasped. My cheeks flushed with embarrassment. This wasn't part of the lesson plan.

His eyebrows rose in amusement as I gave an experimental tug, dragging his hands along with mine.

"Trust me, the pleasure is all mine," Brontes laughed, the rich sound rolling through his broad chest.

I bit my lip, contemplating how to free us. "Let me try something," I whispered, focusing my storm powers to generate warmth in my fingertips.

As the heat radiated from my skin, the ice melted away. Our hands remained locked together, now slick with water instead of encased in frost.

"Fixed it," I replied, my voice barely audible as I reveled in the feeling of our entwined fingers. The warmth seeped into every pore, mingling with the electric charge that always accompanied our touch.

Brontes chuckled deep in his throat, his eyes studying me intently. "You're just full of surprises, aren't you?"

He leaned in closer, his warm breath caressing my cheek. I nodded, nuzzling against the crook of his neck. Just being close to him made me feel safer, his familiar scent enveloped me—a mix of sandalwood and electricity that made my heart race.

"You are intoxicating," he breathed out, leaning down to nibble at my earlobe.

I gasped, arching into the touch, unable to resist his magnetic pull any longer.

Brontes kissed me fiercely, claiming my mouth with his tongue, tasting me thoroughly as if he'd been starving for this moment.

"Brontes . . ." I moaned softly into his mouth as he palmed my breast through the thin fabric of my nightdress, desire coiling hot and tight within me.

Our tongues danced eagerly together. In between our hungry and passionate kisses, he grasped the hem of my sheer nightgown, drawing it up and over my head in one smooth motion. I sat before him naked, suddenly self-conscious under his smoldering gaze. Sensing my hesitation, he gently cupped my face in his hands.

"You are so beautiful, my queen. Let me remind you how much I adore every inch of you."

His words dissolved the knot of anxiety in my chest. I needed him . . . needed to relinquish control and trust Brontes to chase away my worries, if only for a few blissful hours.

He bore me backward onto the bed, the familiar pressure of his strong body both exhilarating and comforting at once. Our hips pressed against each other, igniting a spark within me. I could feel his arousal through his clothes, making me wet with need.

He sat back to remove his own clothes. My eyes drank in the sight of his muscular body, lingering on the hard length jutting out from between his legs.

"Tell me what you want," I whispered, feeling bold and empowered by the effect I had on him. "Tell me how to please you, my king."

Brontes made a low noise of approval, desire darkening his eyes. I lay bare before him, flushed with need and trembling with anticipation.

"Touch yourself," he ordered, guiding my hands to rest on my breasts.

His eyes followed the curve of my fingers as they gently glided over my breasts. He licked his lips, watching intently. I kneaded and caressed them into erect points that begged for attention. My head fell back, and soft moans escaped from between my lips. His breathing turned into gasps for air as I pleasured myself. He couldn't tear his eyes away. The sight of me following his orders, willingly submitting to him, only served to heighten his arousal.

"More," he demanded through gritted teeth, his hands gripping my hips tightly. Obediently, I spread my legs for him, exposing my core.

I dipped my fingers between my thighs, sliding them gently back and forth to coat them in my heat. As I moaned again, lost in the sensation of my own touch, I relished the effect of my actions on him—his erection throbbing against his stomach, beads of sweat running down his muscled chest.

Brontes growled and straddled me. He trailed hot kisses down my neck and collarbone, nipping gently at my skin.

"You have no idea how much I want you." He suddenly pinned both of my wrists above my head, causing me to gasp, and fiercely consumed my left breast in his mouth. He swirled his tongue around the sensitive bud before sucking it greedily. One hand continued to hold my wrists down against the bed, and the other hand roughly pinched the sensitive peak of my right breast between its fingers.

"Brontes!" I writhed helplessly beneath him, aching for more of his touch.

As he continued his assault on my breasts, I freed my hands and traced the heated lines down his abdomen until I reached his firm manhood. Brontes sucked in a sharp breath as my fingers encircled him. His eyes closed with bliss as I ran my hand up and down his throbbing length slowly, deliberately. I increased my pace, savoring the way his body trembled and quaked beneath my touch.

A low grunt rumbled in Brontes's chest, and he abruptly grasped my hand. "Enough teasing, or I won't last."

He stroked the inside of my thighs as I stilled underneath him before zeroing in on the throbbing spot between my legs and kneading it in circles. I gasped from his masterful touch. His fingers found my entrance and circled slowly, teasingly. My cold fingers kneaded his shoulders, digging into his skin, urging him on.

I gasped for air as he pushed two fingers into my folds, then three, stretching my tightness. My body begged for more, clenching around them and demanding he delve deeper. He pulled back and growled, his lips finding my neck as he worked his fingers in and out of me with shifting rhythms, leaving me guessing at his next move.

I wanted him. I needed him. I ached for him . . .

"Brontes," I moaned, "make love to me."

"Oh, I will. I'm going to make love to every inch of you. I'm going to make you scream. I'm going to make you beg. And you are going to love every second of it."

"I already do," I responded softly, my eyes drifting closed.

Brontes kissed me fiercely, settling between my legs.

"Make me yours, my king," I firmly commanded, gazing into his eyes.

He entered me with one smooth thrust, stretching and filling me so exquisitely that I cried out.

We moved together, slow and deep, savoring the intimacy of our joining. His muscles rippled beneath my fingers as I gripped his scarred back. His skin was hot against my cool touch, the friction from our movement creating a scorching heat. The coil of desire in my belly tightened with each roll of Brontes's hips, pleasure building and intensifying until I thought I might burst.

"Brontes," I murmured, "I'm so close."

"Tell me what you need, snowflake," he panted, his firm hands raking over my breasts and torso.

"Harder," I begged.

My pulse raced as he complied. Thrusting faster and harder than ever before, his hips moved with an urgent rhythm that made my body tremble, driving me closer and closer to the precipice.

"Let go, my queen," he urged, his gaze locked on mine, willing me to surrender to the ecstasy that awaited us both.

And so, with a final cry, I abandoned all restraint and allowed myself to be swept away by the tide of our passion. Our bodies moved as one, our minds connected on a level that transcended the physical realm. Warmth flooded my core as Brontes found his release, filling me with his seed and tipping me over the edge into euphoria.

As we lay there, tangled in each other's arms, the afterglow of our encounter enveloped us like a warm embrace. After a little while, Brontes brushed a stray lock of hair from my face, his touch now gentle and tender.

"How about some more training, snowflake?" He smiled adoringly. "I need to practice my new ice powers, and you need to teach Helena too."

"I *hope* I can teach her." I nibbled my lip nervously.

"You will, but hopefully her lesson won't end like ours did." He winked. "If it does, can I watch?"

"Brontes!" I swatted his chest playfully, cheeks flaming.

He just chuckled.

"So . . . I need to think of something that makes me feel *dead* inside?" Helena asked me and Brontes skeptically.

"Yes, something like that," I replied with an uncertain shrug.

"Okay . . ." She nodded thoughtfully. "I'll give it a try."

We were back in the gym, the boys occupied in the corner.

Helena closed her eyes, brow furrowing. "What makes me dead inside?" she muttered.

Her face smoothed into detached calm. She inhaled deeply before thrusting her hands forward.

Nothing happened.

I sagged in disappointment, but Helena persisted. "Almost had it. One more try . . ."

She repeated the process—eyes shut, breath held, hands extended—but this time . . .

A glossy sheet of ice spread across the floor!

"Yes! Well done!" I cheered. "What did you think about?"

Helena laughed sheepishly, flicking her wild red hair behind her shoulder. "An awful history exam Fannar and I took. Bored me to tears!"

Our laughter was cut short by a tremendous crash shaking the building's foundations.

In a blur, Fannar appeared between us, one hand on my shoulder and the other on Helena's back. Brontes positioned himself between us and the door. Both of them were protective as always.

"What the hell was that?!" Helena cried out.

An ear-piercing siren began blaring, causing me to jump.

"Is that an emergency alarm?" Brontes shouted over the noise.

Helena nodded grimly. "Last time it went off was when Fannar's parents sent a yeti to kill me."

The ceaseless alarm grated on my nerves. "What should we do?" I chewed my bottom lip.

Fannar hesitated. "Usually, we're supposed to go to the gym, but we're already—"

Before he could utter the last word, the wall beside us warped and bent. We recognized the sign now—the precursor of a Cosmic Enchanted's portal forming in our presence.

"Brace yourselves!" Brontes shouted.

We flared our powers in our hands, ready to fight back. But instead of Obsidia, Headmaster Moira stepped through the shimmering portal.

"Good, you're all here," she said briskly. "Come to my office at once."

We quickly rushed through the portal, a swirl of purple and green energy surrounded by a black outline. When we stepped through, my stomach churned and my skin tingled as we emerged on the other side.

"Headmaster, what's happening?" Fannar asked once we were all in her office.

The administration building trembled violently under deafening rumbles caused by an unseen force. A few terrified screams drifted from outside.

Headmaster Moira glanced up at the ceiling urgently. "She's here. My defensive shield won't hold long against another Cosmic Enchanted. I cannot allow her to endanger the remaining students and the academy."

"What do we do now?" Helena asked.

After considering it briefly, she gave us an enigmatic smile. "As they say, desperate times call for desperate measures." Headmaster Moira rolled up the long sleeves of her deep purple dress above her elbows and extended her arms outward. "Pay attention, students. You're about to witness something most never will."

The building quaked again, even more violently, rattling me to my bones.

The time had come to take a stand.

CHAPTER SEVENTEEN
HELENA

The office trembled violently around us, books and trinkets tumbling from shelves. I grabbed Fannar's arm to steady myself as the floor bucked beneath our feet, my ears ringing from the thunderous crashes.

Brontes, however, sprinted for the window and gaped at whatever lay outside.

"Gwyneira, look at this!" he cried.

Gwyneira raced over to the window and gasped in shock at what she saw. She whirled around to face us. "We're in space!"

"What?!" I exclaimed.

"There's a binary star system swirling around us!" she replied, her eyes wide, unable to contain her excitement.

"Really?" Fannar gasped. He moved toward the window, and I followed, my curiosity overcoming my concern.

An endless expanse of inky blackness met my eyes, deeper and vaster than any night sky. It was a light-devouring abyss, pierced only by the fiery pinpricks of distant stars. Swirling nebula clouds glowed softly, billowing strands of violet, pink, and teal.

Headmaster Moira had indeed transported the administration building of the academy into space.

A blaze of scorching heat washed over my face, even through the glass. A blinding streak of light shot downward, leaving trailing afterimages in my vision. Moments later, a horizontal bar of blinding radiance seared my eyes right to left.

"What was that?" I asked breathlessly.

"A binary system with two orbiting stars," Gwyneira responded with awe. "I've never seen one up close before!"

"More importantly, it's protecting us," Brontes added. "Look, Obsidia can't get past it."

I followed his pointing finger. In the distance, a hazy violet aura marked the location of the Cosmic Enchanted as she hovered amid the celestial fury.

"Students!" Headmaster Moira called sharply.

We'd nearly forgotten about her in the commotion and hurried back to where she stood, her features taut with strain. I'd never seen her looking so haggard. Perspiration beaded her brow, and her eyes were bloodshot. Even her hands trembled slightly.

"Listen closely," she said, low and urgent. "Just as I anticipated, Obsidia followed us here in pursuit of all of you, but even Cosmic Enchanted can't stay in space for very long. She's using a tremendous amount of her energy just to survive right now. Hopefully, her magic will become weak enough for you to defeat her." Headmaster Moira paused to take a ragged breath.

"Do our powers even work in space?" Fannar asked.

"Of course, they do," the headmaster replied. "Your powers come from within, regardless of your environment."

"But what if Obsidia comes after you?" I asked.

"I'll be fine. I've placed a shield around the building so only the four of you can come in and out and created a bubble of artificial gravity around it. In case of this very situation, I also imbued stones granting thirty minutes of artificial gravity and cosmic protection for survival in space." The headmaster nodded toward her desk. "They're in the top drawer. You must defeat Obsidia before their power wanes"—her gaze dropped to her shaking hands—"or before mine does."

As Brontes moved to fetch the stones, I watched in horror as a crimson droplet trailed from the headmaster's nose. The evidence of her own failing strength made my heart clench with fear.

What will we do if we can't defeat her in time?

"Um . . ." Gwyneira interjected. "Shouldn't we contact Aria and the other kingdoms that offered their assistance?"

"There's no time," Headmaster Moira explained. "It's not possible for me to teleport anyone else here and protect the academy at the same time. You'll have to face Obsidia on your own."

"We won't let you down," Fannar declared staunchly.

Headmaster Moira smiled faintly at his words. "Please be safe, all of you. I wish I could offer more aid."

Brontes distributed the stones, smooth black ovoids that glimmered mysteriously. They looked just like the stone the headmaster had used to look into my memories.

Since Brontes and Gwyneira had never seen an enchanted stone before, I explained, "Press the swirl in the center to activate it."

They both nodded, examining their stone closely. I rubbed my thumb over the carved spiral on mine, feeling the hum of magic.

"Are we ready?" Fannar asked solemnly.

"Do we all remember the plan?" Brontes added with an edge of urgency.

My breath hitched as panic coursed through me. Every muscle in my body tensed up, and my stomach clenched so tightly that it threatened to heave.

Brontes had outlined the plan only once, and the complex details blurred into a jumbled mess in my mind.

"Yes," Fannar stated with steady confidence.

Gwyneira shot me a sidelong glance, wringing her hands nervously. "I think so."

Uh . . . I literally only summoned ice once a few minutes ago! How can I possibly be ready for a cosmic battle?

I had no idea if I could remember the plan, but I nodded hesitantly anyway. It was do or die, so there was no point in voicing my doubts now.

"Then let's go!" Brontes said.

He led the charge toward the main doors, the rest of us on his heels. As he flung them open, a violent vacuum threatened to suck us into oblivion. We instantly activated the space stones, nullifying the deadly pull.

Brontes took the first cautious step outside. A glowing violet disk materialized under his foot—Headmaster Moira's magic creating translucent "stepping stones" in the void.

He turned back to us. "It's working!"

I trailed after him, mesmerized by the violet stepping stones materializing beneath my feet. Behind me, Fannar and Gwyneira quietly followed suit.

The void of space stretched out around us, a vast expanse of frozen stillness. Stars twinkled in the distance like tiny pinpricks in the fabric of the universe, their light barely reaching us. My heart raced in anticipation of what was to come, the impending showdown with Obsidia. The moment felt heavy with suspense, as if the universe waited for somebody to make the first move.

"Let's move!" Brontes urged. "Thirty minutes until the stones expire."

We broke into a sprint toward the Cosmic Enchanted.

Obsidia noticed our approach, alarm flashing across her beautiful face. We'd caught her off guard.

"Stick to the plan!" Brontes reminded us firmly. My mind raced, trying to recall the intricate strategy.

"I see that you're working with that hag Moira," Obsidia sneered. "She can try protecting her beloved academy, but she can't protect you!"

Obsidia thrust her hands forward violently. Space dust recoiled from her strike in a shuddering pulse. Ready this time, I threw myself clear of the shockwave.

"Phase one, now!" Brontes yelled.

Right. Ice attacks first. Feel dead inside . . .

The lecture hall came into my mind, the history exam in front of me, ticking clock, shuffling papers, stifling silence. Utter mind-numbing boredom.

My emotions flattened in response. I fixed Obsidia with a glacial stare and flung my palms out. Jagged shards of ice materialized, swarming toward her. Beside me Fannar did the same, multiplying the frozen onslaught.

"You think these pathetic tricks can defeat me?" With a snarl, Obsidia dispersed the volley of ice. But Fannar and I continually replenished them from all sides, hemming her in.

"Phase two!" Brontes shouted.

Fannar and I veered away. Brontes and Gwyneira replaced us, conjured a massive tornado, swirling with sharp ice particles, around the Cosmic Enchanted. Obsidia's screams echoed strangely as the whirling shards sliced her with countless cuts.

"Get out of my way!" she shrieked furiously, finally bursting free.

"Retreat!" Brontes barked.

We turned and fled, luring her after us over the spiked rooftop of the building. Brontes and Gwyneira laid down obscuring veils of frosted fog as we ran.

Obsidia pursued, spitting curses. "No you don't. I won't fall for this again!"

When she paused to blast through their frozen clouds, we were ready. Fannar and I ambushed her with jets of fire, swallowing her in a blazing inferno. Her agonized howls were chilling.

But with a burst of power, Obsidia surged through the flames straight at us.

Shit! She's supposed to run away!

Before we could react, her hand clutched Fannar's throat in a vise-like grip.

"You can't defeat me!" she hissed. "You're not even a Cosmic Enchanted!"

Rage boiled within me. I launched myself at Obsidia, cracking a kick against her ribs. She gasped, releasing Fannar. Her magic flickered erratically as she tumbled backward.

"Phase three, now!" Brontes yelled.

Phase three . . . that's the storm attack!

"Ready?" Fannar asked, turning to me.

I nodded, steeling myself. "As ready as I'll ever be."

We unleashed a torrent of flames upon Obsidia, but she matched us strike for strike. Her wild eyes stayed locked on us as we dueled.

Brontes and Gwyneira quietly crept forward. The plan was for them to ambush Obsidia from behind while

Fannar and I kept her distracted with our attacks. If only it had been that easy.

"Four against one isn't fair. But don't worry, how about I even the odds a little?" Obsidia smirked.

Before they could reach Obsidia, she braced both of her hands. Instantly, the surrounding space grew heavy and cold, vibrating with an eerie hum of magic. A dark ball swirled between her palms, bolts of black lightning snapping from its center.

"Let's see how you fulfill the 'Storm of Fire and Ice' prophecy if I put out the fire first," she taunted menacingly.

Obsidia unleashed the sphere of deathly energy, a crackling menace of darkness hurtling through the void. Its pure malevolence seemed to warp reality, leaving a trail of frigid emptiness in its wake.

My eyes widened in horror, and a cold sweat prickled across my skin as I realized her attack was aimed directly at me. There wasn't enough time to dodge the blast. All I could do was throw up an ice shield as quickly as possible and hope I would survive.

"NO!" Fannar's voice tore through the air like a whip.

My vision narrowed as Fannar zoomed toward me with superhuman speed. In one powerful leap, he sent himself hurtling through space. Before I could figure out what he was doing, he barreled into me, knocking me out of the way like a rag doll.

The raw power of Chaos Magic slammed into him with the force of a meteor, catapulting him backward helplessly.

The sickening crunch of stone and bone reverberated through space as he collided with one of the administration building's tall spires. Chunks of stone and slate broke free, plummeting downward like violent confetti.

Fannar's broken body left a crater in the spire. He tumbled down the wall, his motion marked by a trail of blood that followed his descent until he lay motionless in an unconscious heap of scorched flesh and smoke at the edge of the roof.

"FANNAR!" I screamed. My heart hammered in my ears as I sprinted toward him, the enchanted stone creating stairs up to the roof. My vision tunneled to focus solely on his crumpled form.

"BROTHER!" I barely heard Gwyneira's muffled shriek behind me.

Every other sound and sight fell away. All that mattered was reaching him. I crossed the shimmering shield that encased the building. As I neared, the dark energy continued to crackle around his body for a few moments until the black tendrils snaking over him finally disappeared.

"Oh, my God," I choked out, dropping to my knees beside him. "Fannar."

The full extent of his injuries became horrifyingly clear. His clothes were charred and tattered, barely clinging to his body, revealing singed flesh beneath. The blast left an angry, blackened trail across his chest, marring the once smooth surface with gruesome burns. My stomach twisted as I fought back the bile rising in my throat.

Fannar's chest rose and fell in a weak, ragged rhythm, each breath seeming to take all the strength he had left. He struggled for every inhale, and it tore at my heart.

"Helena . . ." he whispered, wincing as he tried to move before gazing up at me through pain-clouded eyes.

"Shh, don't move," I insisted, brushing my fingers lightly over his singed hair. "Save your strength, Fannar. Everything's going to be okay."

"You . . ." he rasped, his gaze locked on mine, "you need to . . . stop Obsidia."

"No, I need to get you help!" I snapped, my fear for him turning into anger. "Headmaster Moira can take us back so we can get you to the Healing Center."

"No, Helena . . ." he said through his bloodied lips, his voice weak and strained. Fannar's eyelids fluttered ominously.

"Stay with me, Fannar," I whispered fiercely, fighting back tears. "You have to stay with me."

"Go, finish it." Then his eyes slid closed as he succumbed to darkness.

CHAPTER EIGHTEEN

GWYNEIRA

A terrifying, primal, brutal, savage howl. The sound of pure rage.

I hardly recognized the raw, guttural cry of my anguished scream as it tore through the astral void.

"BROTHER!" I couldn't breathe. My heart pounded against my ribs as my eyes locked onto Fannar's broken body. Blood pooled beneath him, a bright crimson against the black tiles of the roof where he lay.

"Foolish Prince," Obsidia mocked. "Oh, well. I needed him dead anyway." Violet flames wreathed her hands as she gathered herself for another attack.

Not this time.

A storm ignited inside me. My anguish had taken form, a chaotic whirlwind of emotion and power tumbling inside me, and I couldn't hold it back any longer.

Never had I felt such blistering fury. I embraced it. Fed off it. Fueled by it. I would avenge my brother or die trying.

Ice crystallized along my body as rage kindled a fire in my veins. I strode toward her, a torrent of ice shards swirling violently around me like a protective barrier. The cold bit at my cheeks, freezing the tears trailing down them, but I welcomed it. The chill focused my rage.

Focusing on the powerful storm tearing within me, I released an electrifying blast from my hands. It struck Obsidia with a loud scream, her smug expression replaced with an agonized grimace.

"Gwyneira?" Shock flickered in Obsidia's voice. "That was you?"

My answer was another bone-jarring lightning blast.

Obsidia steadied herself, regarding me with a new wariness. "I see you've finally grown a backbone, little mouse. Pity it won't save you. Once you're dead, Brontes will be mine!"

Lightning split the air, its electric tendrils illuminating Obsidia's twisted grin as shards of ice hurtled toward her like lethal daggers. My heart thundered in my chest, a furious drumbeat matching the frosty tempest I'd unleashed.

"Ah, your anger is simply *adorable*," Obsidia taunted as she effortless deflected my attack.

"Shut up!" I spat, my breath turning to frost as it left my lips. The storm within me seethed, fueled by the desperate need to avenge Fannar and punish our tormentor.

"Gwyneira!" Brontes yelled, scrambling toward me, his hands aglow.

"Stay out of this, darling," Obsidia ordered as she released a bolt of Chaos Magic from her fingertips, sending Brontes flying back with its force.

"Brontes!" I screamed, watching him spin through the dark void and struggle to regain his footing.

Oddly enough, I was secretly grateful for Obsidia's obsession with Brontes. She wanted him alive.

"You'll pay for that!" I roared, my anger multiplied tenfold. I charged at Obsidia, imbued with a strength I'd never felt before. Lightning crackled in my veins as I unleashed a barrage of ice and lightning at her, forcing her to retreat.

"Gwyneira, stop!" Brontes's voice echoed in my mind, cutting through the maelstrom of my thoughts, but I hardly heard it. All that mattered was the powers coursing through my veins and the need to bring Obsidia to her knees.

Arctic tendrils of rage snaked through me as I unleashed a relentless assault. An electric hum filled the air, alive with the energy of the storm I'd summoned. Bolts of ice-spiked lightning tore through the sky, each strike aimed at our malevolent foe. Blast after blast, I gave her no time to recover or gloat. Each step I took closer to her was punctuated by another jagged bolt of icy lightning.

Sweat trickled down my temple, stinging my eyes, but I refused to give in. This was no time for weakness. I persisted, discharging another torrent of ice and lightning, until I completely lost sight of her, blinded by my own ceaseless lightning.

As my vision cleared, Obsidia floated before me, unscathed.

"Is that all you have, princess?" Obsidia taunted. A black hole swirling from the Black Rose Brooch absorbed my last of my attacks.

A chill of dread suddenly shot through me. I gasped as her hand clamped around my throat.

"Impressive, little mouse," Obsidia purred. "You're the first Ice Princess I've encountered that isn't cowering behind someone else. Such a pity I have to kill you, anyway."

Obsidia's face filled my vision, luminous yellow eyes boring into mine. "What? No sniveling pleas? No begging for your life?"

"You . . . will . . . never win," I managed to grumble out, meeting her gaze squarely. If these were my final moments, I would not cower or repent.

Her grip around my neck tightened. "Too bad you won't be here to find out!" Obsidia sneered, her voice a sinister echo in the cosmic expanse.

Tendrils of darkness began to mar my vision. This was it. I had fought with everything I had. If Fannar didn't make it, we would reunite soon. I only wished I had more time with . . .

Brontes . . .

A thunderous roar split the abyss. Obsidia shrieked as a massive lightning bolt knocked her backward, releasing me as she reeled into space. I gasped air desperately into my starving lungs.

Brontes lunged forward, murder blazing in his dark eyes. "Get away from her, bitch!"

Another crackling bolt erupted from his palm straight at Obsidia, causing her to back away.

"Gwyneira, are you okay?" Brontes lifted me to my feet and guided us behind the headmaster's shield.

"I'm fine." I rubbed my throat, bracing myself to make the next move. "We need to end her."

"Wait, Gwyneira!" Brontes grabbed my wrist. I whirled around toward him, ready to unleash my wrath. But his eyes locked onto mine, full of fear and desperation, concern etched in every line on his face. "You can't keep this up! You'll exhaust yourself. We have to be smart about this."

My chest heaved as I glanced at Fannar's battered form. Helena was kneeling over him. It didn't look good. My heart thumped in my chest like a war drum.

"We can't let her get away with this," I gritted through my teeth, despair threatening to suffocate me.

Brontes shook his head. "We won't, but we need a better strategy."

His hand encircled mine. His touch momentarily calmed the tempest within me.

"Fine," I conceded. "How do we take this witch down?"

Electricity sparked from our hands as we stood there, locked in our desperate search for a solution. The taste of ozone lingered on my tongue. Obsidia's cruel laughter still rang in my ears, her taunts echoing through the void.

"The prophecy," Brontes muttered, his eyes narrowing as he dug into his memories.

"The one she keeps talking about?" I asked.

"Yes, the Storm of Fire and Ice . . . that phrase. It might be the key!"

"She does talk about it like she's trying to prevent it from happening."

"Think about it, Gwyneira." Brontes glanced at me eagerly. "Storm, fire, and ice—that's us! Our powers combined!"

"That's why she's been trying to get rid of me and Fannar, so there wouldn't be ice."

"And she just tried to get rid of Helena so there wouldn't be fire."

My mind raced as I stared up at him, uncertainty gnawing at the edges of my thoughts. Was it possible? He seemed so sure, and the look in Brontes's eyes that made me want to believe him. Could it be true? The idea seemed preposterous, almost too simple . . . yet a tiny flicker of hope kindled within me.

A Storm of Fire and Ice could be our salvation, hidden in plain sight.

"Remember what Headmaster Moira told us?" Brontes continued. "In the face of chaos, unity and balance are your greatest weapons."

I nodded. "If we're going to defeat Obsidia, we must harmonize our elemental powers."

"Right!" His eyes lit up with excitement. "Let's get Helena."

We darted toward the roof of the administration building.

"Giving up so soon!" Obsidia cackled from the other side of the shield, her laughter echoing in my ears like nails on a chalkboard.

We had to figure out how to summon the Storm of Fire and Ice. The fate of Fannar and our world hinged on it.

CHAPTER NINETEEN
HELENA

The eerie darkness of the void surrounded me, appearing to never end. I tenderly caressed Fannar's cheek, willing him to open his eyes. His skin was unusually hot to the touch.

Gwyneira and Brontes drifted closer, their faces etched with determination. Stars shimmered in the distance, casting a somber glow on Fannar's unconscious form. I clutched his hand tightly, fear knotting my stomach. Each second that ticked by felt like an eternity. His labored breathing filled my ears, making the severity of his condition all too real.

"Guys, he's hurt badly!" I said, panic welling up within me. "We need to get him out of here. Tell Headmaster Moira to take us back to the academy so we can get him to the Healing Center!"

"Helena." Gwyneira's soft voice barely cut through the silence. "We can't."

“What are you talking about?” I snapped, my grip on Fannar’s hand tightening. “Fannar needs help. I don’t know how much longer he’ll last.”

“There’s something else we need to tell you.” Brontes exchanged a glance with Gwyneira before he spoke. “We think the Storm of Fire and Ice is how we can defeat Obsidia once and for all.”

My heart hammered in my chest as I barely processed his words. “I don’t care about Obsidia! Fannar needs help NOW!”

“This might be our only chance to stop her,” Brontes explained firmly but sympathetically. “Now that Obsidia has fallen for it once, Headmaster Moira won’t be able to trap her in space again. This is our best shot at defeating her with as few causalities as possible.”

“Are you serious?” I stared at him incredulously and then turned to Gwyneira. Surely, his sister would understand. “You too, Gwyneira? You want to leave Fannar like this?” I gestured to his pale face, his shallow breaths the only sign of life.

“Of course not, Helena!” Gwyneira’s eyes filled with tears as she looked at her brother, but she didn’t waver. “My heart feels like it’s being ripped apart seeing him like this. But Brontes is right. If we don’t end this now, she'll stop at nothing to conquer all our kingdoms, and countless lives will be lost. We have to try."

Heat surged through my veins as anger flared within me. My mind raced, torn between my love for Fannar and this ridiculous responsibility that was thrust upon me. How could they ask me to choose between saving him and stopping Obsidia from destroying the Enchanted Realm?

Did I even care about a world without Fannar in it?

"Do what you want!" Furious, I gritted my teeth, trying to control the fire threatening to burst forth. "I'm staying with Fannar."

"Helena, we need you." Gwyneira said gently, touching my shoulder.

"The Storm of Fire and Ice needs all three of us—storm, fire, and ice," Brontes explained. "With Fannar down, you are the only one with fire."

"I'm not leaving," I snapped, my voice raspy and strained. "I won't let him die alone!"

The admission of those words—that Fannar was indeed dying—pressed down on my heart like a million suns. A tear streaked down my cheek as I stared at him, his chest barely rising.

"Helena—" Gwyneira began.

"I can't . . . I love him so much." My voice cracked. Tears flowed from my eyes as my heart twisted with guilt. "He was protecting me. I can't just leave him like this!"

"Helena, I love him too." Gwyneira's eyes filled with empathy. "I know how deeply you care for my brother, but please ask yourself, is this what Fannar would want? Do you truly believe that Fannar would want us to abandon our duty to the realm? To let Obsidia win?"

Her question pierced through me like an icy dagger. Duty above all else. That was his way, wasn't it?

I looked away, not wanting to answer Gwyneira. As I leaned over to gaze at Fannar's pale face, the phoenix pendant that Etheri had given me swayed back and forth from my neck. Its fiery wings spread wide, a silent testament to the resilience and the spirit of my mother that coursed through my veins.

"Never forget the spark that lives inside of you," Etheri said.

My fingers curled around the pendant. The spark inside me seemed to burn brighter, fueled by the memory of Aria's words about how she overcame the Iron Circle's dark magic. *Love, trust, and balance.*

Could those words guide us now, as they had guided Aria through insurmountable odds? I closed my eyes, allowing that phrase to engulf me. Love for Fannar, yes.

But also trust in our friends and balance between duty and heart. A lump formed in my throat, and I clenched my fists, trying to keep the flames of anger and fear from flickering to life in my hands.

Opening my eyes, the path was clear. I refused to let Obsidia win. She had messed with the wrong Combined Enchanted.

"You're right," I said through my tears, clutching what was left of his shirt. "He said to stop Obsidia. 'Go, finish it.'"

"That sounds like Fannar." Gwyneira gave a small bittersweet smile.

"Fine," I choked out, struggling to keep my voice steady. "But I don't want to leave him here on the roof. It's not safe."

"Agreed." Brontes nodded solemnly, his face betraying a mix of relief and sadness. "I'll take him inside the building. He'll be safe with the headmaster behind her shield."

I nodded, blinking back tears. "You better hang in there, Fannar," I whispered to him as I caressed and kissed his cheek one last time. "You have to fight. I'm going to fight like you asked, so you better fight too."

Gwyneira reached for her brother's hand and gasped as she felt his scorching skin. "He's burning up. We have to get him cooled down." Her hands waved over Fannar's body a few times, wrapping him in a thick cocoon of ice. "Hopefully, that'll help stabilize him for now." Then, she spoke directly to Fannar. "It's your turn now. Like you always told me, brother, be strong."

For a few moments, we stood in silent vigil around Fannar before I finally nodded. It was time to go. Brontes carefully lifted Fannar and carried him inside the administration building's protective walls while Gwyneira and I followed close behind.

When Brontes returned outside, I whispered one last silent prayer for Fannar's survival. And with a deep breath, I stepped away from the one I loved, hoping fate wouldn't force me to leave him behind forever.

"Alright," I said, my voice stronger and more determined now. "How do we create this Storm of Fire and Ice?"

"We don't exactly have instructions," Brontes replied.

"I think we just need to combine our powers together, even our second Combined Enchanted powers," Gwyneira ventured.

An ominous rumble echoed off the shimmering barrier surrounding the building, heralding Obsidia's approach once again.

"Come out from behind that shield and fight me, you cowards!" Obsidia taunted us. "I'll be sure to reunite you with your Ice Prince in death!"

She would pay for what she'd done. With a loud cry, I thrust forward and unleashed a barrage of scorching fireballs that successfully drove Obsidia back, if only for a moment.

Brontes, Gwyneira, and I stood, rooted like ancient trees to the violet platform beneath our feet, ready to face her once more. The cosmic void swirled around us, uncertainty hanging heavy in the air as we prepared for what might be our final stand. The three of us—storm, ice, and fire—were all that stood between Obsidia and the destruction of everything we held dear.

Obsidia's sinister laughter echoed through the emptiness of space.

"Let's end this," I said through gritted teeth.

"Are you ready?" Brontes asked.

"Ready," Gwyneira replied firmly.

Our gazes locked, and our hearts pounded in sync as we grasped each other's hands. I closed my eyes and reached for the fire within me, the familiar warmth pulsing like a second heartbeat. Beside me, Brontes's power roared to life, electricity crackling in the void. Gwyneira's ice spread beneath our feet, cool and unwavering like her quiet strength.

But as we tried to manifest our secondary powers, something felt amiss. The connection between us wavered, unsteady as a newborn fawn. My brow furrowed as I realized that Gwyneira's hands easily swirled with voltage, but it was Brontes and I who were struggling. Both of our ice abilities refused to manifest at will.

"Come on!" I hissed, frustration mounting.

"Dammit," Brontes cursed.

But the more I tried, the more doubt crept into my mind. My mind whispered words of failure and inadequacy, reminding me again that I barely just used ice for the first time. *Can you even do this, Helena?*

The dissonance between us grew, threatening to sever our bond entirely.

"Helena, Brontes," Gwyneira declared softly. "We can do this. We've fought too hard to give up now."

Her words washed over me like a balm, soothing the doubts that gnawed at my heart. I nodded, my resolve renewed, and once again reached for my powers.

My left hand ignited with orange and yellow flames, while a chill ran up my right arm, wisps of frost floating into space. Across from me, sparks of electricity danced between Brontes' fingers, and ice crystals glittered around him.

This time, though, Obsidia's brassy eyes narrowed as she recognized our plan. "Arrogant children," she sneered, her voice dripping with malice. "You have no idea who you are up against."

With a flick of her wrist, our surroundings warped and twisted as her powers took hold. The headmaster's shield was failing. Thick inky smoke billowed forth, obscuring our vision and filling my lungs with a choking heaviness. Vivid phantoms swirled at the edges of my vision—nightmarish shadows come to life. They couldn't be real . . . could they?

"Don't lose focus!" Brontes bellowed. "Be strong for Fannar and our kingdoms."

With a shout, he summoned a gale that tore through the smoke and dispelled the illusions. The shadows retreated, their taunts fading into whispers.

Our wills intertwined, weaving into a rope of resolve as our combined might vibrated through the vastness. I tightened my grip on their hands and that invisible thread connecting us, its power pulsing around us like a cyclone.

"Love, trust," I murmured.

"Unity," Brontes said.

"Balance," Gwyneira said.

Our bodies began to glow with bright auras: fiery red for me, icy blue for Gwyneira, and electric yellow for Brontes. They began to blend seamlessly, melding into a kaleidoscope of color.

The boundaries between us evaporated, three becoming one, creating a symbiotic tapestry of strength that stirred the very fabric of space around us. Our elements wove together in a whirlwind of unseen forces.

"Whoa," I breathed, watching the celestial tableau take form before us.

A Storm of Fire and Ice.

It was an angry vortex of razor-sharp shards of ice, filled with deafening bolts of lightning, and streams of fire shooting from its core. Vibrant colors streaked through the abyss as space itself seemed to tremble, charged with our Combined Enchanted elements.

"Are you guys feeling this?" I asked.

"Every fiber of my being," Gwyneira's eyes glowed bright blue as her powers intensified.

"Let's turn it up a notch!" Brontes shouted.

With each surge of energy we poured into the tempest, it grew more potent, more relentless, becoming an unstoppable force that defied the laws of nature.

"How is this possible?" Obsidia snarled with disgust.

The winds howled in concert with our combined might, and I could see the fear in Obsidia's eyes as she realized the extent of our strength. She had underestimated us, and now she would pay the price.

"I think it's time we finished this," Brontes smirked at us with a gleam in his eye.

Gwyneira and I nodded at each other.

"Let's do it," I said.

Brontes's eyes locked on Obsidia. "NOW!" he roared.

And together, we unleashed a supernova of elemental fury, magnifying our powers beyond anything we could achieve alone, that shook the heavens. The sky split with a deafening roar, echoing across dimensions as the unstoppable maelstrom surged forth, seeking to engulf Obsidia completely.

Violet and ebony streaks of lightning flew from her palms, forming a protective dome over herself to defend against the tempest we created. The Black Rose Brooch pinned to Obsidia's chest flared to life in a gruesome luminescence. Tendrils of Chaos Magic snaked from the brooch to strengthen her shield.

"You think your little parlor tricks will stop me?" she mocked. "You aren't powerful enough to summon the Storm of Fire and Ice!"

The maelstrom of lightning, sparking embers and icy shards swirling within, bombarded her barrier. Despite her best efforts, the cyclone grew closer as it slowly consumed her shield.

"It's over, witch!" Brontes declared. "Surrender now or be destroyed!"

"Give up!" I yelled over the deafening roar of the storm. "It's over!"

"Never!" she vehemently bellowed, her face twisting in fatigue, her eyes blazing with defiance. "It's my destiny to rule the realm with Brontes!"

"Then this is your end!" Gwyneira's eyes flashed with ice-cold rage, her normally gentle voice as hard as steel.

With that, we pushed the Storm of Fire and Ice into the black barrier, ready to deliver the final blow.

The Black Rose Brooch throbbed eerily in tandem with Obsidia's cosmic powers as she summoned more Chaos Magic to add to bolster the shield's strength.

But our vortex advanced forward, waves of Combined Enchanted power peeling away each layer of her sinister defenses.

"Don't let up!" Brontes growled through gritted teeth, his arms outstretched as if he were physically thrusting the storm toward Obsidia. "Keep pushing!"

"Got it!" Gwyneira shouted beside me, her pale blue eyes reflecting the violent ballet of fire, ice, and storm.

"I'm pushing!" I called back, my heart pounding wildly in my chest. My body ached from the strain of sustaining such immense power, but I refused to falter. Not when we were so close to victory.

"We're almost there!" Brontes urged, his eyes locked on Obsidia as she struggled against the elemental onslaught.

Suddenly, Obsidia's protective dome exploded in a brilliant flash of purple and black light . . . and then it was gone.

"NOOOOO!" she screamed with pain and disbelief.

For a fraction of a second, I saw her standing tall, her head held high and eyes burning with hatred. The Black Rose Brooch was now dull and lifeless, having lost the Chaos Magic that once fueled it.

With a final primal roar, the full force of the Storm of Fire and Ice lunged at Obsidia, sweeping her up in wrathful waves of fire, ice, and lightning. Her eyes widened in terror, but there was no escape. She thrashed and flailed like a rag doll in its punishing grasp.

"Argh!" Her shrill screams echoed but soon faded, lost in the deafening crack of lightning and roar of flames, as the onslaught of elemental fury engulfed her like a ravenous star.

A poignant void of silence stretched across the vastness of space, punctuating the end of the elemental fury. The Storm of Fire and Ice gradually dissipated, the ghosts of our combined powers echoing in the void left behind.

Obsidia's body floated limp and motionless, the malevolent glow of her brooch extinguished, her once unruly power now reduced to a wisp of steam.

"Is it . . . over?" Gwyneira asked hesitantly.

"It seems so," Brontes replied, nudging Obsidia's lifeless form. "She won't be harming anyone else."

I cautiously inched forward, staring in astonishment at her broken figure, a strange mixture of comfort and surprise washing over me.

"We did it," I murmured, disbelief still evident in my voice.

This was it. The prophecy was fulfilled. Obsidia was truly defeated. After all her boasts of conquest, her physical form would be lost in the unending expanse of space forever. I almost pitied her. She never understood the power that came from fighting for something greater than oneself.

We won. Our kingdoms were now safe. United, not just in power, but in love and trust.

A sense of stark relief and pride settled in my heart, but I couldn't dwell long on our victory.

"We need to get Fannar to the Healing Center."

CHAPTER TWENTY
GWYNEIRA

"When two stars in a binary system orbit near each other, their gravitational forces can affect the outer layers of their atmospheres," I read aloud from a book titled *The Orbit of Binary Stars* at Fannar's bedside. "In some cases, these close binaries can transfer mass between them, allowing them to reach stages of evolution that single stars cannot reach."

Glancing up from the book, I realized Fannar's eyes had drifted closed, his chest rising and falling with each steady breath. With a soft smile, I closed the book and set it aside. In the tranquility of sleep, the lingering toll of his injuries was less obvious on his face.

The soft orange glow from the crystals cast a warm light over the Healing Center as I sat in a carved wooden chair, surrounded by a gentle symphony of beeping monitors. The tranquility of the room enveloped me as the sweet scent of lavender and rosemary caressed my senses.

A gentle hum of energy vibrated through the air, blending with the sound of Fannar's breathing.

I pressed the back of my hand to his cheek lightly. His skin was cool now, the fever finally broken. It had been touch and go there for a while after the battle with Obsidia. I shuddered remembering how weak he'd been, how the light in his eyes had dimmed. But he was ever resilient, and with the care of the academy's healers, he slowly recovered. We had almost lost him, but he was still with us.

The past few days, Helena and I had barely left his side, taking turns watching over him, reading to him, entertaining him, making sure he ate, and simply just being there. I knew that our doting could be a little overwhelming and even embarrassing to Fannar, who remained the stoic prince despite his brush with death. But I could tell that he truly appreciated our love for him as he gathered his strength, even if he didn't say it out loud.

Now seeing him resting peacefully, his face smooth and untroubled, my heart filled with gratitude for having been able to be part of my brother's healing journey. The nurse said he should be discharged soon, right before winter break ended and Brontes and I would need return to the Storm Kingdom.

Fannar stirred, his icy blue eyes blinking open. He looked at me, a frown forming on his brow.

"Why'd you stop reading?" he asked, his voice still groggy from sleep.

I giggled softly. "You fell asleep, my dear brother. I didn't want to disturb your rest. Besides, it seems that you don't share my enthusiasm for binary stars."

"What do you mean? I obviously find it fascinating." Fannar gave a faint smile. "But it was nice to hear your voice. It's . . . comforting to know you're here, sister."

"I'm glad I'm here too." I squeezed his hand. "Helena will be here soon. You can ask her to read more to you."

Fannar let out a chuckle. "If she reads that, she'll fall asleep sooner than I will."

I laughed in agreement, my heart swelling with relief at seeing him regain enough strength to laugh. "It's funny how you two are so different. But in many ways, you're perfect for each other, you know. You're both incredibly strong . . . and incredibly stubborn!"

"Tell me about it," Fannar said with a scoff.

"You know, after you were hurt, she refused to leave your side, even when it meant risking letting Obsidia win," I recounted, my admiration for her growing with each word. "She was willing to sacrifice everything for you, brother. Brontes and I had to convince her to finish the fight."

"I know." He had heard the story before, but he still stared at me, the vulnerability clear behind his eyes. "I can't believe she would do that. I mean, I'm mad she would consider it—risk the whole realm's safety for me. But . . . I can't blame her either. I've never met anyone like her."

"Neither have I," I agreed, feeling a warmth spread through my chest. "Do you think Helena's the one?"

Fannar didn't hesitate, a small smile tugging at the corners of his lips. "Yes, I do."

I beamed, feeling a surge of excitement for their future together. "That's wonderful, brother! She will be such an amazing Ice Queen. Unique and powerful, unlike any in our kingdom's history."

Fannar nodded, a tender smile touching his lips. "Thank you for convincing her to fight. I know it wasn't an easy decision for you either." He squeezed my hand, his voice raw with emotion. "I can't even begin to tell you how proud I am of you, sister," he said, his voice raw with emotion. "And of Brontes too. You all showed incredible bravery and courage."

"Thank you, brother," I replied, touched by his words.

"My baby sister defeated a Cosmic Enchanted!" Fannar declared triumphantly. "And pretty soon, you're going to be the Storm Queen."

Just then, the door burst open, and Helena rushed in. Her face lit up when she saw Fannar awake.

"You're up! How are you feeling?" Helena asked breathlessly, hurrying to his side. Her fiery curls bounced around her shoulders as she peered down at him, her green eyes filled with concern and love.

Fannar's face softened. "Much better, thanks to you both." He took Helena's hand in his.

I smirked at them. "Fannar wants you to read more from this book about binary stars."

"Really?" Helena's expression dropped as she held out her hands to take the book. "Oh. Okay . . ."

"I'm just kidding!" I giggled.

She flashed a big grin. "Funny."

"I'll give you some time alone," I said. "See your later, brother."

"Thanks, sister."

As I left the room, I glimpsed Helena leaning down to kiss Fannar tenderly. My heart warmed by their obvious devotion and knowing my brother and I had both found happiness.

The brisk wind whistled through the courtyard, rustling the leaves and tossing my long white hair across my face. We stood in a semi-circle around Headmaster Moira, her long black dress whipping around her in the breeze. Our eyes fixed on her as we awaited the reason behind this impromptu meeting.

She surveyed the four of us with a stony expression, her lips pursed, as if she had something she wanted to say but couldn't quite bring herself to do it. Finally, she cleared her throat and spoke.

"I have called you all here today for a reason," she began, her usual calm voice tinged with unease. She gingerly opened her hand to reveal the Black Rose Brooch. Its onyx petals glimmered in the faint light. "I'm afraid the Black Rose Brooch may still pose a threat."

My breath caught in my throat.

"What?" Fannar exclaimed.

"Shit," Helena cursed.

"But I thought we destroyed it!" Brontes said.

The headmaster shook her head. "Its power has merely been suppressed. Given time, it could regenerate."

My stomach twisted. After everything we suffered at Obsidia's hands—the battles, the destruction, almost losing Fannar—the lingering threat of the brooch still loomed over us like a dark cloud. My hands trembled at the thought.

"So what can we do?" Fannar asked.

"I've been thinking about it for the past few days." Headmaster Moira's gaze firmly locked onto the evil artifact in her hand. "I suggest that we break apart the Black Rose Brooch and scatter the pieces throughout the Enchanted Realm. This way, it can never be reassembled. But I want your agreement since it was the four of you that worked together to defeat Obsidia."

The headmaster's words hung in the air, and we all looked at each other, our faces mirroring the same sentiment: determination to destroy the Black Rose Brooch once and for all.

"Sounds like a solid plan, Headmaster," Brontes spoke first. "Whatever it takes to protect the realm."

"Agreed," I added. "We can't let anyone else suffer because of that cursed brooch."

"Yes." Fannar nodded, his expression resolute. "We've come too far to let that thing fall into the wrong hands ever again."

"Do it!" Helena slammed her fist into her palm.

Headmaster Moira gave a satisfied nod. "Excellent," she said. "Be ready, students. Magic is capricious, and I can never say how it will turn out."

We followed her advice and stepped back cautiously, ready to defend ourselves should things not go as expected.

"Let's begin." She raised her hands.

The wind whipped around us as she summoned her Cosmic powers. The Black Rose Brooch floated into the air before her, glinting ominously in the pale winter light. We all watched with bated breath as her eyes focused intently on its ominously intricate design.

A wave of violet energy emanated from her hands, and the brooch trembled and cracked. I flinched, half expecting some eruption of dark energy. But the fractured brooch simply hung there, inert and powerless, devoid of the evil power it once held.

My breath caught in my throat as the sound of shattering glass filled the air. The brooch splintered into hundreds of tiny pieces all at once.

As Headmaster Moira kept her hands pointed toward the floating shards of black glass, countless small portals began appearing all around us, swirling vortexes of light suspended against the gloomy sky.

"To the deepest oceans, the highest mountains, the driest deserts, the densest forests, and across the farthest reaches of the Enchanted Realm," the headmaster spoke solemnly. "May you find your final resting places, never to be found again."

With a flick of her wrist, an invisible force drew every fragment into a portal until they had all disappeared out of sight.

As the last portal closed, Headmaster Moira surveyed each of us, her gaze soft yet stern. "Thanks to all of you, the fragments of the Black Rose Brooch are now scattered across the realm, and Obsidia will never threaten us again. You have shown yourselves worthy of becoming the future leaders of your kingdoms."

"Thank you, Headmaster," we murmured with reverence.

A spark of hope and anticipation surged through me as I gazed upon Helena, Fannar, and Brontes. The four of us represented half of all the kingdoms. Together, we would usher in a new era of peace and unity for the Enchanted Realm.

Helena and Fannar exchanged tender glances and intertwined their hands. My eyes drifted up to Brontes, who had been a pillar of strength throughout this ordeal. Through everything, he resisted Obsidia's dark temptations of unparalleled power and conquest of the entire realm. He demonstrated that his unwavering love and goodness was a light that could not be extinguished.

I linked my arm with his, leaning into him with tears of joy pricking at my eyes. A deep contentment infused my bones. Here, wrapped up in Brontes's embrace, was my happy place. No kingdom or crown could ever mean more to me than this man's love.

"You're thinking too loudly," Brontes murmured, his lips brushing my hair. "What's going on in that beautiful head of yours?"

I smiled, tilting my face up to meet his gaze. "Just realizing how lucky I am to have found you."

His eyes softened, filled with a tenderness that made my heart ache with joy. "Without you, I would have become the tyrant that Obsidia knew. I'm the lucky one, my snowflake."

A tear spilled down my cheek, and he reached up to brush it away, his thumb caressing my skin with an almost reverent touch that sent a delightful tremble through me.

This was all I ever wanted—a love to stand the ages.

"Promise you'll never stop loving me," I whispered.

"I would sooner stop breathing." He pressed a soft kiss to my lips. "You are mine always, and I am yours."

I sighed, enveloped in bliss and the security of his vow. The sun peeked out from behind the clouds, shining as brightly as the future Brontes and I would forge together. Always and forever, against all odds, our love would endure.

CHAPTER TWENTY-ONE

GWYNEIRA

Three months later

"You may now kiss the bride!" The officiant's words resonated through the air.

Adorned in his black military uniform, the medals and gold buttons gleaming like stars, Brontes looked every bit the regal king he was destined to be. His heavy gold crown rested upon his head, a testament to his responsibility and unwavering strength. As he pulled me close, the warmth radiating from his body enveloped me in a cocoon of profound love.

The depths of his navy blue eyes captivated me, like gazing into a star-strewn midnight ocean. Deep, boundless blue. Everything else faded away, leaving just the two of us standing there, lost in each other's presence. He was all I could see in that moment, and I wanted that moment to last forever.

Our lips met in a tender, passionate kiss, sealing our union beneath the moonlit glow. I lost myself in the sensation, my heart swelling with unbridled joy and affection for this man who had stolen my heart and awakened my soul. My fingers gripped against the rough fabric of his uniform, a stark contrast to the tenderness of his embrace.

As Brontes pulled away from our long, loving kiss, the applause and cheers of our audience filled my ears, bringing me back to reality.

That's right. We have an audience.

The Storm Castle gardens had been transformed into a majestic wedding venue for the exchange of our sacred vows. We stood under a trellis draped with white roses, wisteria, jasmine, and camellia. The sweet perfume of delicate flowers mingled intoxicatingly with the earthy scent of pine and cedar of the surrounding trees. Each blossom's stem was lovingly wrapped in ribbons of shimmering gold and sapphire blue. They lined the aisle in abundance, their pale petals almost glowing under the starry night sky.

Behind the officiant, the pond shimmered and glistened as the light of the stars twinkled in its rippling surface. The serene water mirrored the heavens above, creating an ethereal atmosphere, as if the entire Storm Kingdom weaved their powers together to make this night perfect.

My snow-white wedding dress sparkled with a thousand iridescent hues in the moonlight, its delicate and sheer fabric shimmering like a million tiny diamonds, as if it were a thin sheet of ice. The sleek bodice fitted to the contours of my body, with crystalline patterns decorating the sleeves and gown that mimicked the frost on a window on a cold winter morning.

Perched atop my pale locks, a magnificent tiara shimmered in the moonlight, its bright white diamonds and deep sapphire stones glimmering like starlight. Intricate swirling patterns of snowflakes, thunderbolts, and tiny stars adorned its delicate gold frame, symbolizing the union of ice and storm being joined together in marriage.

Helena and Maisol stood by my side, their bridesmaid dresses reflecting the elegance of the night. Helena's fiery personality seemed to be momentarily contained by the soft blues and golds that adorned her gown, while Maisol's nurturing demeanor complemented her flowing dress, its colors reminiscent of a winter's dawn. Both ladies gently blotted tears of happiness from their eyes.

Opposite them, Fannar and Cid, the captain of the Storm Knights, cut striking figures in their own ceremonial dress uniforms, standing tall and proud beside Brontes. My brother's presence there, blessing my marriage to the man I adored, was a gift beyond measure. The two most important men in my life side by side.

In the front row, my parents looked on, their usually stoic expressions softened by the pride gleaming in their eyes. It warmed my heart to see that their reserved nature could not entirely mask their joy for me. A few of my former handmaids, as well as Fannar's closest servants from the Ice Castle, sat behind my parents, who had allowed my favorite handmaid, Adis, to relocate to the Storm Castle and become my personal assistant.

Sadly, Brontes's parents were absent by necessity, not choice. When it became excruciatingly obvious they wouldn't change, Brontes made the difficult decision to permanently transfer them from the castle dungeons to the official prison. Despite the pain it caused him, he made that choice for the betterment of his kingdom and the future we would build together. I hoped on this day he would only feel love surrounding him.

Also in the front rows were the Storm Castle's loyal servants turned dear friends, including Rori, Dagur, Elias, and Nana Osborne. Their smiling faces reminded me that this grand occasion was also intimate, shared with those who had nurtured our love. Brontes and I had given all the castle servants the weekend off to celebrate our wedding as guests, and my parents had graciously loaned some of their Ice Castle staff to assist with hosting the festivities.

Dignitaries from all over the Enchanted Realm honored us by their presence, including Headmaster Moira, the kings and queens of the Air, Water, and Earth Kingdoms, Helena's sister Princess Aria, Asher, and members of the Fire Council. Their attendance, transcending elemental and territorial boundaries, gave Brontes hope that the peace he had always wished for could someday become a reality.

Behind the faces of our gathered loved ones stood the formidable Storm Castle, resilient in the face of adversity, and fully repaired since Obsidia's attack. Brontes insisted that it should be even taller and more grandiose than before, adding a touch of ice to its design so it would truly embody the union of ice and storm.

Brilliant glass towers and tall spires glistened in the light as they stretched to the sky. They rose from the imposing black spiked fortress, intertwining with the original Gothic architecture in a graceful waltz, a beautiful dance of opposites. The outlines of various glass walls and crenellations were lit with a soft blue glow. I marveled at how our elements not only complemented each other but strengthened one another as well.

As part of the renovations, the servants' quarters were relocated into the east wing of the castle, upgraded from what was essentially a rickety barn to proper bedrooms shared by no more than two servants each.

The officiant, a wise magistrate who was now one of Brontes's most trusted advisors, cleared his throat, bringing me back to the present. He smiled benevolently at us both. "Ladies and gentlemen," he began, his voice echoing through the serene garden, "I now present to you, His Majesty King Brontes and Her Majesty Queen Gwyneira of the Storm Kingdom."

Our friends and family erupted in cheers and applause. As I took in the beloved faces surrounding us, my heart overflowed with joy and profound contentment. This was more than just a wedding. It was a testament to the power of love and unity to bridge vast differences. Here, in this very garden, we had forged bonds transcending bloodlines and kingdoms.

Once more, I glanced up at the celestial sky above. The stars twinkled like diamonds against the inky blackness, mirroring the boundless possibilities that awaited us. A sense of hope and wonder permeated the atmosphere, wrapping us in the comforting embrace of love and harmony.

"Ready for forever, my queen?" Brontes beamed at me, taking my hand.

"More than ready, my king," I replied with a smile.

We strolled up the aisle arm-in-arm, smiling brightly and our eyes twinkling with joy, while delicate white rose petals fluttered down from above us like a gentle summer shower.

Bound before the gods forever as husband and wife, king and queen, Brontes's heart was mine, and mine was his, for all our days together under sun, stars, storms, and snowfall.

CHAPTER TWENTY-TWO

HELENA

Throughout the entire wedding, Fannar fought to keep a stoic face, though his struggle to contain his emotions was adorable. He fought back tears when he first saw Gwyneira glide down the aisle, her sparkling gown transforming her into an ethereal vision. As the couple exchanged heartfelt vows, gazing adoringly into each other's eyes, Fannar's composure nearly shattered.

By the time Brontes kissed his bride, most of us were sobbing. Even Fannar's eyes glistened, though he valiantly held back the flood.

As we followed the newlyweds toward the Storm Castle for the reception, I sidled closer to Fannar. His face was an expressionless mask, his mind in a distant place.

"You okay, babe?" I asked gently.

Fannar's icy eyes met mine briefly before skittering away. "Hmmm . . . I'm not sure," he admitted.

I slipped my arm around his waist comfortingly. "It's a big day for you both."

He nodded. "She looked so happy up there with Brontes. He's a good man, and now she's a *queen*! I'm thrilled for her, truly." Fannar's voice dropped. "It just didn't fully sink in until now that she won't be coming home again."

My heart ached for him. For all Fannar's composure, saying goodbye to the sister he'd protected for so long couldn't be easy.

"She doesn't need me anymore," he said with a rueful chuckle. "My little sister's all grown up now."

"Hey, she'll always need her big brother," I assured him. "She'll visit us, and we can visit the Storm Castle anytime."

Fannar just shook his head, smiling sadly. "You're right. I'm being silly . . ."

I stopped, turning him gently to face me. "It's a big deal. I love that you care so much about her."

Cupping his cheek, I drew him down until our foreheads touched. We stood that way in silence until Fannar's taut frame relaxed.

"Helenaaaa!" Too soon, the tender moment was broken by an ear-piercing squeal.

I whirled around just in time for the source of the noise to crash into me. "*Iris?!*"

"Helena!" My roommate shrieked again as she rushed in for a hug with her boyfriend, Guiden, trailing behind her. "Oops, is it Helia now?"

"Helena is fine," I said, laughing and shaking my head.

"My gods, you look so gorgeous!"

"How are you here?"

"Fannar invited us!"

My eyes darted to Fannar, who already seemed a little cheerier at the sight of our friends from the academy.

"Surprise." Fannar flashed a coy smile at me.

"Oh, my God!" I exclaimed, clutching Iris's hands in mine.

"Everyone is so pretty! I've never been to a royal wedding before!" Iris shrieked as we both bounced up and down with delight.

Beside us, Guiden gave Fannar a hearty pat on the back. "I hope your spring break hasn't been as exciting as your winter break, my friend. No rogue Cosmic Enchanted trying to take over the world?"

"Fortunately not." Fannar chuckled lightly. "Just helping Gwyneira with the wedding preparations."

"It's unbelievable that your sister's wedding brought guests from every kingdom." Guiden's eyes widened in awe as he took in the scene. "This is amazing!"

"It's all amazing!" Iris exclaimed. "*You're* all amazing, but"—she cut herself off and squealed in excitement again—"I can't wait to see the inside of the Storm Castle!"

Guiden rolled his eyes with a little smirk. I laughed. The historic peaceful representation of every kingdom of the Enchanted Realm in one place was nothing compared to a party in a castle in Iris's eyes.

"Let's go!" Iris grabbed my hand and started running.

"Iris!" Guiden called.

"Hey!" Fannar shouted.

She dragged me behind her as she sprinted. All I could do was laugh and wave at the boys' dumbfounded faces as they realized they would need to chase us. Iris and I cackled as we pelted down the courtyard, full of energy, in our kitten heels.

Ready to party.

The castle had been lavishly transformed for the reception. Music floated through the opulent halls as we arrived. The air carried the fragrance of white flowers that adorned the Grand Hall, intermingling with the sweet scent of the Storm Castle's cherry wood carvings. Iris immediately dragged me gleefully onto the dance floor before most guests had even entered. We claimed it as our own, twirling deliriously beneath the sparkling lights long after others drifted away.

Gwyneira and Brontes moved gracefully across the marble floor of the Grand Hall, sharing their first dance together. She was an ethereal vision. Her gown sparkled like a million stars in the night sky with its soft, shimmering illumination. I never managed a private word with Brontes or Gwyneira, as the newlyweds constantly found themselves mobbed by well-wishers. But Fannar stole a treasured moment with his radiant sister while I shouted my congratulations over the crowd surrounding the couple.

When Iris allowed us to take a break from dancing, we indulged in an exquisite mix of unique culinary specialties. We devoured the savory flavors of the Storm Kingdom, such as steaming slabs of honey-basted beef ribs, succulent roasted birds, and mulled cider. Then, we delighted in sweet delicacies from the Ice Kingdom, like crystallized frost-berry treats, colorful marzipan fruits, and ice wine.

The wedding cake itself was a spectacular marvel, crafted by Gwyneira's friend Maisol as a precise replica of the Storm Castle. Each tower was expertly sculpted and piped with swirls of buttercream frosting to perfection. Edible gold dust gave the walls a soft shimmer that glint in the light. Adorable fondant figures of Gwyneira and Brontes stood proudly atop the castle, complete with diamond-like sparkles reflecting from their eyes.

Fannar and Guiden joined Iris and me on the packed dance floor, and the four of us danced with carefree abandon, losing ourselves in our own world of music and movement. My cheeks glowed and feet ached from exertion. But my heart felt light, filled with nostalgic joy. For a few hours, I simply existed as Helena again. Not a Combined Enchanted. Not a princess of the Fire Kingdom. Not the girlfriend of the future king of the Ice Kingdom. Just a college student embracing the night with her boyfriend and closest friends as music and laughter swirled around us.

Tomorrow our duties—and our studies—would return. But for now, I reveled in this celebration of love and friendship.

As I haphazardly folded my clothes and packed them into my bag, I hummed one of my favorite songs from Brontes and Gwyneira's wedding reception the previous night. The afternoon sun streamed through the window, casting a warm glow over the guest room that Fannar and I shared in the Storm Castle.

Anticipation bubbled in my chest at the thought of returning to the Ice Castle with Fannar. We were going home the next morning.

I stopped in my tracks, taken aback by the fact that I just referred to the Ice Castle as "home," even if it was in my mind.

Home.

A smile tugged at the corners of my lips. The word felt as comforting as the sun that bathed my face.

The place had once felt so cold and uninviting. But now, when I pictured the icy turrets of the castle glinting in the sunlight, an inexplicable warmth spread through my chest. Fannar's home had become mine as well.

After that witch leveled the majestic Ice Castle to the ground, a new citadel arose from the ashes, entirely transformed from what it had been before. On the outside, it still retained its ethereal beauty, appearing as a magnificent structure made of pure ice. But inside, Fannar's parents ensured that the castle was now equipped with heating and warm insulation.

When Fannar questioned them why, they simply answered, "So Helena won't be so cold."

How were they the same people who had sent a quad-eyed yeti to kill me after hearing of our relationship? I couldn't believe how far we had come. Their kind gesture moved me to tears and spoke volumes, symbolizing their acceptance of me as part of Fannar's life and the Ice Kingdom's future.

As I continued packing, my heart filled with gratitude for being accepted by Fannar's family. It was an invaluable gift to be welcomed into their world, a nod of approval for our love.

The sound of a light tap on the door stirred me from my musings. A timid-looking young servant girl poked her head inside, carefully glancing downward out of respect.

"Your Royal Highness Princess Helia," she said, "His Royal Highness Prince Fannar requests your presence in the library."

"Thank you," I replied, curiosity bubbling up in me. Why would Fannar want to meet me in the library?

As I made my way through the ornate corridors of the Storm Castle, each step heightened my anxiousness. What ominous discovery did they make in the library: the return of the Iron Circle, another relic of Chaos Magic, or yet another Obsidia from a different timeline? My skin turned cold and the hairs on my neck stood straight as the worst possibilities spun in my mind.

As I pushed open the heavy oak doors, the library greeted me with warmth and comfort. The high, vaulted ceilings were adorned with intricate frescoes depicting mythical creatures and enchanted landscapes. Thousands of books lined the towering shelves, their spines boasting various hues that seemed to dance in the flickering firelight. The inviting scent of aged parchment and leather bindings filled my nostrils, somehow soothing my restless spirit.

My eyes spotted Fannar standing by the fireplace, his tall, athletic frame silhouetted against the crackling flames. His arctic blue eyes locked onto mine, sending a jolt to my core. He extended his hand, beckoning me closer. The surrounding air hummed with an electric charge, drawing us together like magnets.

"What's going on, babe?" I asked with a light laugh, absolutely puzzled.

"Helena," Fannar began, his voice low and tender, "I brought you here because it reminds me of all the times we spent together at the academy library. Those whispered conversations as we studied and our stolen moments together . . . They hold a special place in my heart."

As he spoke, my heartbeat quickened from the unknown. What was he getting at?

Fannar gently took both of my hands in his, and I could feel the love radiating from him. The fire crackled softly in the background, casting flickering shadows across his chiseled features, making him even more handsome than usual.

"Our journey together has been filled with unexpected twists and turns. We've faced everything from a Fire douchebag who wouldn't take no for an answer, my parents trying to murder you, rescuing my sister who didn't actually need rescuing, learning you're a long-dead princess, and finally my near-death at the hands of a rogue Cosmic Enchanted." He paused, a soft smile gracing his lip s.

I chuckled lightly, a joyful tear escaping my eye, recalling those irreplaceable and some horrifying memories we shared.

Fannar brushed the tear away with his thumb, his eyes never leaving mine. "But every moment has only strengthened my love for you. I cannot imagine a life without you by my side, as my best friend, my partner, and my queen."

Then, to my astonishment, he knelt before me, revealing a beautiful ring shimmering in the firelight. My breath hitched as I realized what was happening.

"Princess Helia of the Fire Kingdom, will you marry me and rule by my side as the next Ice Queen?"

Joyful tears pricked my eyes as I stared at Fannar in disbelief. Was this really happening?

"Uh, Helena?" Fannar prompted, still on one knee.

"Yes, of course I'll marry you!" I cried.

Fannar's face lit up with relief and elation. He stood and slipped the ring onto my finger.

The ring's flame-shaped gold band gleamed in the light, resembling liquid gold, while masterfully set around it were twelve fire opals in a brilliant red-orange hue, infusing the ring with the vibrant life of blazing fire. A snowflake pattern encased a magnificent icy-blue diamond in its center, with each point of the starburst design adorned by sparkling white diamonds. Amazement washed over me as I took in how flawlessly this piece of jewelry captured the blend of fire and ice.

"Do you like it?" he asked hesitantly.

"It's perfect!" I buried my face in his chest, overwhelmed with happiness, as he pulled me into a tight embrace.

After a long moment, I tilted my chin up to look at him again. "Shouldn't we wait until after we graduate to get married though?"

Fannar shrugged. "Maybe, but I couldn't go one more day without asking you."

I grinned. "I'm happy you did . . . but now our studies and training are that much more important since we're going to be ruling a kingdom together!"

"I was always planning to rule a kingdom." He chuckled and tenderly brushed a strand of hair from my face as he held me by the fire. "But if you want to focus on graduating first, that's what we'll do."

I nodded. "Is that okay? I don't want to be a shitty queen."

He released an uproarious laugh and then looked down at me with his icy eyes full of tenderness. "Don't worry. Just knowing you're mine forever will make every day worth the wait."

My heart filled with love for this man who wanted so much for me to stay by his side. "And you're mine. Through everything, no matter what comes." I raised my lips to his.

Our kiss was soft at first, tender even, but it quickly intensified. The warmth of Fannar's lips against mine made my heart skip a beat as I leaned into him. I clung onto him tightly as he kissed me deeply in the front of the roaring fireplace of the library. The contrasting sensations of fire and ice mingled, creating an electrifying heat that coursed through my entire being. His presence brought the essence of winter, and his crisp snowy scent blending with the earthy smell of aged books only heightened my excitement. My hands found their way into his hair, reveling in its silky texture.

Fannar's fingers traced the curve of my collarbone, causing goosebumps to rise on my skin that had nothing to do with the chill of his powers. His lips moved to my neck, trailing soft kisses along the column of my throat as his hand slid down to grip me firmly in his. I gasped at the sensation, arching into him as he explored every inch of my skin with his lips and tongue. His touch was like a cool breeze on a sweltering day, refreshing but biting all at once. Heat built up inside me, spreading like wildfire through my veins.

"You're so warm, Helena," Fannar groaned, moving his hand to my thigh.

Another moan rose from the pit of my stomach as his hand moved higher, tracing the inside of my thigh. I wanted nothing more than to feel him against me, to lose myself in the moment. My fingers dug into his shoulders, urging him on, and he let out a low chuckle against my skin before pulling away slightly. Our eyes locked, and for a moment, all I could see was desire burning in those icy depths. He leaned in again, capturing my bottom lip between his teeth in a gentle nibble.

"We should go back to our room." Fannar's husky voice mirrored my own growing desire.

"We should," I uttered breathlessly as I stepped away from him and locked the library door. I shot him a coy smirk. "But where's the fun in that? It's not like this'll be the first time we've done it in a library."

He hesitated for a moment, his icy blue eyes searching mine.

"I want you here. Now." I bit my lip seductively, my pulse quickening.

"So naughty." Fannar's gaze darkened, and his lips found mine again in a searing kiss that set my senses aflame.

His arousal pressed against me, and my own desire pulsed in response, aching to be sated.

"You have no idea how much I want you," he murmured, his breath hot against my skin.

"Show me," I challenged, my pulse racing as Fannar's lips descended upon my neck, teeth nipping gently at the sensitive flesh there.

Fannar's large hands ran over my body, his touch igniting a fire within me that burned brighter than any flame I could conjure up. He moved his hands up my sides, down my arms, and across my chest, sending shivers of delight through my entire being.

"Remember the first time we kissed, and you took off your shirt in the middle of the gym?" he smiled suggestively.

"I remember you left me laying there with no shirt on," I huffed.

His brows furrowed. "Let me make it up to you now."

Suddenly, Fannar grabbed my breasts over my dress and pinned me against the bookshelves. His hands kneaded my breasts vigorously with an almost primal need as his mouth devoured mine. I moaned into the kiss, my hands tangling in his hair to pull him closer.

With a smooth pull, he drew my dress over my head, exposing my breasts to the cool air. I gasped as my nipples tightened, straining against his cold fingers. The contrast between his icy touch and my heated skin sent waves of pleasure coursing through me. His gaze raked over my body, glowing with desire.

"Gods, Helena," he breathed as his fingers dug into my flesh, grabbing my bare breasts in a bruising grip. "I'll never get tired of looking at these."

His hands groped my breasts, kneading the soft flesh roughly and pinching my nipples until tears pricked my eyes. My body ached from the forceful handling, but the sensation only heightened my arousal and fueled my own wild cravings.

"Fannar!" I exclaimed. The combination of pain and pleasure was intoxicating. I ground my hips against his, desperate for friction.

"You like that?" His voice was a husky growl against my ear, bouncing the swells in his hands. "You like when I play rough with these?"

"Y-yes," I whimpered, beyond any other words, the throb between my legs intensifying at his aggressive touch.

He gave them another squeeze and pressed me harder into the shelves, the ridges of old books digging into my back. Fannar's mouth closed over one breast, sucking it with such fervor that waves of pain mixed with pleasure coursed through my body. Teeth grazed my nipple, sharp and sweet, sending a jolt to my core.

My nails scraped into his scalp. He groaned, the rumble vibrating against my breast as he lavished attention on my aching peaks. My head lolled back, my mind a whirlwind of sensations as he moved to my other breast, his tongue teasing before enveloping it completely.

"I can't take it anymore." A throaty moan escaped my lips. The ache between my legs intensified, damp heat pooling as desire unfurled within me.

"What was that?" he asked, pretending not to hear me, his breath hot as his tongue, lips, and teeth continued to assault the sensitive flesh, leaving me trembling.

I cried out, writhing in his hold. Every nerve ending screamed for more—more heat, more sensation, more Fannar.

When he finally released me, my breasts were swollen and throbbing. I clutched at his shirt, trying to steady my ragged breath.

Fannar trailed hot, wet kisses down my neck as his hands slipped between my legs. Moaning softly, I leaned into his hand, my breasts pressed against his chest. The sound seemed to echo in the silent space around us, adding to the sensual tension. My fingers fumbled with the buttons on his shirt, eager to feel his cool skin against mine. As each one gave way, I reveled in the sight of his toned chest and abdomen, all the while breathlessly anticipating the bulge underneath his pants.

But before I could undo them, he grasped my hips and lifted me onto the smooth wooden table nearby.

Fannar smirked, ice-blue eyes glinting as they traced the contours of my legs, leaving a trail of fire in their wake. Then, in one swift movement, he tore off the thin fabric of my panties, sending them to the floor in a tangled heap and baring my sex to his gaze.

"So wet for me already." He nuzzled against my folds, inhaling deeply. "You smell delicious."

I shuddered, equal parts anticipation and embarrassment heating my cheeks.

The cold tip of his tongue drew circles around my bare entrance, causing me to whimper. He chuckled darkly before applying pressure, sliding his tongue inside me slowly. It was like a bolt of lightning, shattering through each nerve ending, and I practically screamed with rapture. His tongue plunged deeper, spinning and investigating, until I felt myself gripping around it.

Without warning, he latched onto my sensitive nub, sucking hard into his mouth and lashing it with his tongue.

"Oh, my God!" I shrieked with legs kicking.

"Come for me," he growled, his voice muffled against my burning core.

His hands gripped my thighs, holding me in place until stars burst behind my eyelids. The pressure built and built until my climax crashed over me, my body shattered into a thousand pieces, my vision whiting out. Fannar continued his assault on my oversensitive flesh, dragging out my orgasm until I was a quivering mess.

Only then did he stand, licking his glistening lips as I lay spread out before him on the library table. The aftershocks of my orgasm still rippled through me as Fannar's eyes locked onto mine, his gaze fierce and hungry. The bulge in his pants was obscene. My chest heaved with each ragged breath, need coiling tightly within me once more.

"Your turn," he commanded, his gaze sultry and intense. His hands had already moved to unzip his pants. "On your knees, wife."

The dominance and possession in his voice thrilled me as I obediently dropped to my knees before him. He pushed his pants down, and his firm erection sprang free before me. I licked my lips in anticipation as I took him in my hand, stroking him slowly.

He eagerly guided my mouth to his engorged manhood, his breath caught in his throat and hips thrusting forward as I took him in. The taste of him was intoxicating, like wintery nights and frozen waterfalls with the sweetness of summer honey. The feel of his swollen skin against my tongue sent sparks of pleasure through me.

"You are so beautiful," he murmured with hooded eyes. He watched me intently, his hand moving down to grasp the back of my neck.

My tongue danced around his length, and then I flicked it against the head. He hissed above me as I did, and I moaned in delight. His grip on my neck tightened, his hips thrusting forward, as he sunk deeper into my mouth. I grew wetter with every passing moment. He groaned above me, his fingers tightening in my hair as I took him deeper, my own moans of pleasure mingling with his. I lavished his hard shaft with broad strokes of my tongue, hollowing my cheeks on each upstroke. His moans filled the room as I sucked and licked, his hands tangling in my hair as I brought him closer and closer to the edge.

"Enough." He abruptly tugged me off him. "I need to be inside you. Now."

He scooped me up into his strong arms and carried me across the room, setting me carefully down on a plush rug in front of a roaring fire. The heat from the flames danced across my skin as he swept his hands through my hair. He positioned himself between my legs.

The blunt head of his member nudged at my entrance, slipping through my wet folds, causing me to gasp. With a wicked grin, Fannar pressed forward, inch by agonizing inch, as he sank into me.

"Fuck!" I hissed at the delicious stretch.

Fannar began to move, slowly and deliberately, allowing me to feel every inch of his girth. His skin was slick with sweat, and his muscles were taut and powerful as he rocked against me. Each thrust sent waves of deliriousness through my body, creating a warmth that spread throughout my being. I arched my back, meeting his thrusts with my own, our bodies moving in perfect rhythm. His hands gripped my hips, reminding me of his strength and stature.

"Helena, you feel so good," Fannar groaned, his grip tightening as he drove into me.

"More, Fannar," I urged. I nipped at his jawline, wanting more of his taste.

He growled low in his throat and withdrew slowly, only to slam back in, wringing a cry from my lips. His hips began a punishing rhythm, thrusting faster, harder, hitting that perfect spot inside me over and over again.

No longer able to keep up, I could do nothing but cling to his back as he pounded into me so deeply I swore I could feel him in my womb. My breath came in ragged gasps. I couldn't believe how good this felt, how much I needed him. I couldn't take it anymore.

"I'm close again," I panted through closed eyes.

And he gave it to me, his hips snapping back and forth in a frenzy.

"Fannar!" I screamed his name.

My body shuddered as the force sent me hurtling over the edge once more. My core clenched around him, milking his masculinity. Fannar threw his head back with a guttural snarl as he reached his peak, spilling his hot seed inside me.

Spent and trembling, we clung to each other on the rug, our ragged breaths filling the library. The world outside our little haven ceased to exist as we basked in the warmth of our shared passion, our bodies still connected.

Fannar exhaled with contentment, pulling me close once more. “I love you, Helena.”

“I love you, Fannar,” I whispered into his chest, watching the engagement ring glint on my hand.

The fire crackled soothingly as we stayed locked in a tender embrace. The future we would build together brimmed with hope and promise. More than any flame, our love burned brighter than ever.

“Shall we go to dinner, my queen?” Fannar asked in a mock formal tone.

“We shall,” I replied, matching his playful voice.

Queen . . . I could get used to that.

EPILOGUE

HELENA

Three years later

T*his is how it ends.*

My body constricted. Slowly crushed to death as I exhaled my last breath.

I'm going to die . . .

"Ow!" I yelped as Iris yanked the corset laces tighter.

"Oh stop, you big baby," she teased. "It's not *that* bad."

I shot her a nasty look in the full-length mirror of my dressing chambers in the Ice Castle. "Easy for you to say! I can barely breathe in this thing."

"Maybe you should have tried it on before *your wedding day*, huh?" Iris just rolled her eyes and gave another sharp tug.

Even in the Ice Kingdom's cold climate, I felt stifled by the dress's cinched corset and unfamiliar textures.

Gwyneira sat on a Victorian chaise lounge chair nearby, watching with concern in her light blue eyes. "Are you sure she's okay? She looks rather pale . . ."

"She's fine!" Iris waved off Gwyneira's worry with an airy laugh. "All brides are a bit dramatic on their wedding day. Gwyneira, hold this string for me."

"Sure."

One more tug. "There!" Iris finally declared proudly and admired her handiwork.

Gwyneira walked around to face me as well. She pressed a hand to her mouth, eyes misting over at the sight of me.

I just grimaced, scrutinizing my reflection. Gilded edging lined the scarlet red dress, with red and orange tulle fanning out from one shoulder while the other remained bare. The bodice hugged my form elegantly, and its intricate gold embroidery depicted a magnificent phoenix rising from the flames. The tight lacing compressed my ribs despite the ornate gold cord crisscrossing up the gown's back. An unavoidable sacrifice for the beautifully dramatic hourglass silhouette it created.

After adorning my fingers, wrists, and ears with jewelry that shimmered like molten gold, Iris crowned my fiery locks with a glinting golden tiara sculpted with even more flames. The ensemble was truly a mesmerizing masterpiece that epitomized the essence of fire. But the vivid crimson hue was a far cry from what I'd imagined for my wedding day.

"It's so . . . *red*," I said with a half-frown.

"Of course, it is!" Iris laughed. "It's a Fire Kingdom royal wedding dress. Every kingdom has their own traditional dress like this."

"You look beautiful," Gwyneira offered kindly.

But uncertainty still gnawed at my confidence. This opulent dress felt like a movie costume, the corset like a torture device. Hardly the ethereal elegance I'd envisioned.

The door creaked open, and Aria glided in, her own ruby gown swishing over the smooth quartz floors.

"How is our bride doing?" she asked with a sing-song voice.

"Your Majesty." Iris bowed reverently at the Fire Queen.

"Stop it, Iris." Aria waved her hand dismissively. "I told you not to call me that!"

Iris smirked. "Never can be too polite."

Aria finally turned to get a good look at me. "Wow, Helena! You look amazing!"

I managed a weak smile. Though tinged with sadness that I wasn't as enthusiastic as everyone else was on my wedding day, their awe sparked a small ember of faith within my chest. Maybe I was just making a big deal out of nothing.

Noticing my ambivalence, Aria rushed over and grasped my hands supportively. "Talk to me. What's going on, little sis?"

I chewed my lip, avoiding her searching gaze. "I just . . . This isn't exactly how I pictured myself as a bride."

"What do you mean?"

I shrugged. "I-I don't know. I always thought I'd be wearing white."

"White?" Gwyneira asked confused. "Like an Ice Kingdom wedding dress?"

"Yeah." Aria nodded at me knowingly. "In the Unenchanted Realm, where we were raised, brides usually wore white wedding dresses, even if they weren't royalty."

"Oh, I see."

"But here, you're a princess," Iris reminded. "You have to represent the Fire Kingdom."

Aria ran a gentle hand over the voluminous red and gold skirts and smiled lightly at me. "This was our mother's wedding dress, you know."

My breath caught in my throat. "It was?"

She nodded. "Yeah, we found it stashed away in an old attic of the Fire Castle after I had already gotten married, so you, dear sister, are the first one to wear it after her."

Our mother should have been here to see this. To hear me tell her how much Fannar meant to me. To plan this crazy royal wedding to the future king of a kingdom that they once considered enemies.

As I twirled from side to side, the skirt billowed and rippled, revealing layers of sheer red, gold, and orange fabric embellished with thousands of tiny crystals. As they caught the light, they created an illusion of flames licking at my heels, making me truly resemble the embodiment of a living phoenix.

I reverently traced the embroidered phoenix, imagining our mother walking down the aisle inside the Fire Castle in this very gown, and touched the phoenix pendent around my neck as I peered into the mirror again.

But . . . she is here now. With me.

"It's perfect," I whispered.

Aria smiled, squeezing my hands.

I took a deep breath, holding it for a few seconds to steady my nerves before exhaling slowly. I stood taller, bolstered. The corset still pinched, but in a new way, like armor girding me for the role I was about to assume. This was my history now.

"Are you ready?" Gwyneira asked.

I nodded with a determined smile. "Let's do this."

Iris let out an excited whoop. "Let's get you married!"

My heart pounded inside the cage of the corset as I nervously waited outside the Grand Hall of the Ice Castle, fidgeting with my gown's gilt trim. Aria, Iris, and Gwyneira's presence kept my panic at bay. As my bridesmaids glided gracefully down the aisle one by one, I peeked through the carved doors, desperate for a glimpse of my waiting groom.

"Deep breaths, Helena," Aria murmured, taking my arm gently. "You've got this."

"Thanks, sis," I replied, squeezing her arm affectionately. "I can't believe this is really happening."

"It's happening!" Aria grinned. "And I'm so glad I can share this moment with you."

"Me too." I clutched her arm tighter.

"You deserve all the happiness in the world."

"Thank you, Aria. I love you, big sis."

"I love you too, little sis."

The doors swung open, and the wedding processional music spilled out into the hallway.

"Ready?" Aria whispered and patted my arm. Her violet eyes sparkled with excitement, a proud smile gracing her lips.

"Ready as I'll ever be," I replied, both anxious and exhilarated at the same time.

As we stepped into the Grand Hall, the splendor within stole the breath from my lungs. It had been lavishly transformed for our nuptials, the polished ice walls and soaring vaulted ceilings glittering with reflected candlelight. Hundreds of flaming sconces lined the walls, their warm glow mingling with the cool radiance emanating from ornate chandeliers of magical ice suspended overhead.

Under their combined light, the hall shimmered as though illuminated by scattered diamonds. I rested a hand briefly over my racing heart, overwhelmed by the fairy tale beauty surrounding me. Soft violin music floated on the air like errant snowflakes.

The spaces between soaring columns were adorned with elaborate sculptures crafted from ice, depicting cherubic figures and mythical beasts. Delicate swirls and whorls covered every frozen surface, capturing the essence of roaring dragons and prancing unicorns in crystal detail. Their frozen forms cast dizzying fractals of rainbow light dancing across the smooth floor, as though we walked through the heart of a prism.

Thousands of delicate fire and ice roses nestled in alcoves all along the walls, their blossoms ruby red, sparkling white, or pale pink all at the same time. The winter roses in hues that perfectly matched my bouquet lined the silk carpet runner unfurling down the center aisle. Their subtle perfume infused the chill air, delicate and ethereal.

As we continued our procession, my eyes scanned the gleeful faces of our guests. Dignitaries from all corners of the Enchanted Realm sat side by side, united on this day to celebrate the love Fannar and I shared. The myriad colors of their attire created a tapestry of unity, a symbol of the harmony that was possible when people put aside their differences and came together.

As Aria and I made our way down the aisle, my eyes fell upon the bridesmaids and groomsmen who stood at the altar. They were like a beautiful rainbow, each one representing a different kingdom and yet coming together in perfect harmony.

Gwyneira stood on the far left of the altar, her pale blue gown gliding effortlessly over the icy floor. The fabric shimmered like the surface of a frozen lake beneath the moonlight. Her black ribbon belt contrasted against the soft hue of her dress, symbolizing the union of the Ice and Storm Kingdoms. The delicate snowflake embroidery sparkled along the skirt, drawing attention to her serene silhouette.

Next to Gwyneira was Iris, my maid of honor, dressed in a stunning green gown that seemed to grow from the earth itself. The intricate leaf-patterned lace clung to her form, cascading into layers of silk that rustled softly like leaves in the wind. She embodied the Earth Kingdom's strength and beauty, a living testament to its lush forests and rolling hills.

At the opposite end of the altar stood Brontes in his black Storm Kingdom military dress uniform. The sleek fabric hugged his muscular frame, while silver lightning bolt accents danced across his chest and shoulders. His dark hair was pulled back, accentuating the storm clouds that always seemed to linger in his eyes.

Beside him was Aspen, Fannar's best man, dressed in the light blue Ice Kingdom ceremonial military uniform. The cool hue complemented his fair complexion, making his bright blue eyes stand out like twin sapphires. The Ice Kingdom's crest emblazoned on his chest, showcasing his unwavering loyalty to both his kingdom and his prince.

At the end of the petal-strewn aisle, a magnificent arch towered over the altar, crafted from shimmering sheets of thick ice, red and white roses teeming for every inch.

By now, hundreds of faces had turned in my direction, but I had eyes only for one.

Fannar…

Fannar stood breathlessly handsome in his own white Ice Kingdom military dress uniform, tailored to fit his strong physique. Silver embroidery danced around the collar and cuffs, like snowflakes caught in a gentle breeze, and a wide silver circlet glinted in his white hair.

As I approached, his ice-blue eyes locked onto mine, filled with so much love and adoration that they outshone the setting sun. In that endless moment, all else ceased to exist. The ornate castle and nobles in attendance faded into irrelevance.

There was only Fannar, the man who had long since captured my fiery heart and restless soul.

The tightness of my corset suddenly became inconsequential. The restrictive embroidery of my crimson gown, a symbol of my heritage of fire, now a comfort rather than constraint.

Though tradition demanded grandeur, we had been joined long before this ceremonial ritual. All that remained was for Fannar to take my hand in his, and for our vows to bless what had always been true in our hearts—that nothing, not even distance or discord, could conquer the love that bonded us to each other since the day we met.

I moved toward my future with my head held high, ready to take my place at Fannar's side, united in purpose and love. Now and forever, my heart's match in spirit and passion.

His lips curled into a smile as he drank in the sight of me from head to toe.

"Wow," he mouthed to me as I stepped closer.

A warmth blossomed in my chest, spreading through my veins like wildfire. A flood of emotions washed over me, love, joy, anticipation, and the tiniest hint of fear.

Aria placed my hands into Fannar's, and the delicious chill from his skin passed through me.

"Take care of my little sister," she said to him.

"I will with all of my being, Your Majesty," Fannar replied firmly.

Aria smiled lovingly at both of us and then took her seat.

Fannar leaned into my ear. "You're so beautiful."

"You too," I whispered.

The ceremony began as I stood with Fannar at the altar, our hands entwined as we faced one another. The priest asked us to read our vows.

"Helena," Fannar began, his voice strong yet tender as he recited his vows, "from the moment I met you, my life has been forever changed. You have taught me what it means to be brave, to face challenges head-on, and to never give up. You've opened my heart to a love I didn't know was possible, and for that, I am eternally grateful. As your husband, I promise to cherish you, to protect you, and love you until the day I die."

His words washed over me like a warm embrace until a tear escape from the corner of my eye. I quickly wiped it away before it could trickle down my cheek.

"Fannar," I said, my voice thick with emotion as I spoke my own vows, "you've shown me what it means to truly love someone, not just with passion but also with understanding and patience. As your wife, I promise to stand by your side, to support you in all things, and to love you unconditionally for all eternity."

The Grand Hall fell into a reverent silence as we exchanged our vows, the power of our words lingering in the air like the final notes of a symphony. Our family and friends had beautiful expressions of pride on their faces, glittering with tears that they blinked back.

"Wonderful," the priest continued, turning to Fannar. "Does Your Royal Highness, Crown Prince Fannar of the Ice Kingdom, take Her Royal Highness, Princess Helia of the Fire Kingdom, to be your wedded wife, to love and to cherish, as long as you both shall live?"

"I do."

"Does Your Royal Highness, Princess Helia of the Fire Kingdom, take His Royal Highness, Crown Prince Fannar of the Ice Kingdom, to be your wedded husband, to love and to cherish, as long as you both shall live?"

"I do."

"By the power vested in me," the officiant declared, "I now pronounce you Crown Prince and Princess of the Ice Kingdom, husband and wife. You may kiss the bride."

As Fannar leaned in, time slowed once more. I took in every subtle detail, from the frigid depths of his icy eyes to the sharp angles of his noble face. My gaze lingered on his pale lips, parted slightly in anticipation of our kiss. At the first tender touch, Fannar's kiss enveloped me in warmth, lingering for what seemed to span lifetimes. Though our rowdier companions hollered and jeered, I paid them no mind. In that moment, there was only Fannar, the scent of pine and frost that was uniquely his, his soft lips upon mine sealed together by the promise of this searing kiss.

When we finally broke apart, the Grand Hall erupted in applause and cheers. Hand in hand, Fannar and I walked back up the aisle to a cascade of white and red rose petals. The love and support of our friends and family propelled us forward as we began our journey together, ready to embrace our future as the next Ice King and Queen with hope, determination, and above all, an unbreakable bond of love.

It's Coronation Day! Witness Fannar and Helena's coronation as Ice King and Queen.

Claim this exclusive bonus scene at:
arielrenner.com/sfi-bonus/

CHARACTER ART

Helena

Fannar

Gwyneira

Brontes

Thank you for taking this journey with Helena, Fannar, Gwyneira, Brontes, and me! You're support means the world to me. ~ Ariel

ALSO BY ARIEL RENNER

Enchanted Realm Prequel

Fated to the Fire Enemy

Haven Academy

Forbidden Ice Prince

Taken by the Storm Prince

A Storm of Fire and Ice

Standalone Titles

My Fated Protector

For up-to-date information on all of Ariel Renner's titles, please visit: **arielrenner.com/books**

LOVE THIS BOOK?

Want more fantasy & paranormal romance from Ariel Renner? Get a free book when you sign up for her email newsletter.

Get your free book now!

https://arielrenner.com/free-book

Printed in Great Britain
by Amazon

39281786R00175